UPSTAGERS

THE HUNTING OF THE SNARK

BOB HESCOTT
STEPHEN COCKETT

D0302068

CollinsEducational

An imprint of HarperCollins*Publishers*

Acknowledgements

The authors and publisher would like to thank the following for permission to reproduce illustrations and photographs:
Popperfoto, main front cover photograph; Central Junior Television Workshop, Nottingham, circular front cover photograph, back cover photograph, pages 67–68; Helen Oxenbury, pages 47–52, 54–55 (top), 84, 90; Liverpool Daily Post and Echo Ltd, pages 54–55 (btm); Imperial War Museum, pages 55, 60; London Fire Brigade, page 57; Local History Centre, Lewisham, London, page 59; Dave Sumner, pages 63–64, 71–74, 76; Donmar Ltd, page 66; Archie Plumb, page 75; The Hulton Picture Company, page 77; Nicholas Greene, page 79.

The authors and publisher would like to thank the following for permission to reproduce copyright material:
BBC Enterprises Ltd © Cable and Satellite Enterprises Ltd 1989, page 79, quotation by Jan Ciechanowski.

Published by CollinsEducational
An imprint of HarperCollins*Publishers*
77–85 Fulham Palace Road
Hammersmith
London W6 8JB

ISBN 0 00 330302 0

First published in 1991

Designed by Dave Sumner
Typeset in Linotron Century Schoolbook by
Northern Phototypesetting Co Ltd, Bolton, Lancs.
Printed in Great Britain by
Bell & Bain, Thornliebank, Glasgow

INTRODUCTION

The play is set in the early years of World War II. Although most children were evacuated, many came back during the 'phoney' war – the quiet period before the fighting and air raids began. Other children ran away and came home under their own steam. Some never went away in the first place.

The bomb sites became giant adventure playgrounds where exciting and grizzly finds could be made. Beryl's find at the beginning of Act Two is a true story. Many children collected the debris of the war – the spent shells from anti-aircraft guns and bits of bomb casings. This sometimes had tragic consequences.

This is a one-set play with most of the action taking place at the 'dig'. The dig is a bomb site which was previously a row of terraced houses.

This is a play about destruction. The set and the characters become more battered throughout the action. At the end, friendship and trust are destroyed. Baker puts his trust in a large bomb and Beaver puts his trust in Butcher who is an ally he neither likes nor feels comfortable with.

The Snark in Lewis Carroll's poem is the hunt for something mythical. Its discovery either solves all the problems for its finders or wipes them out if it turns out to be a Boojum. I have made the Snark of this play a bomb.

Bob Hescott

CAST

THE BRITONS   A street gang, usually just called the 'B's

BELLMAN   Gang leader; intelligent and strong with a sense of fair play

BERYL   A bossy, organising sort of girl

BARMY   A joke within the 'B's; a pathological liar whose lies are always found out

BUTCHER   A bully who would like to be gang leader

BILLIARD BALL   A boy or girl who has had ringworm and is bald as a result; the scalp is always purple from the ringworm lotion

BOXER   A physical boy given to sparring and back slapping; not dangerous

BLAGGER   A cheerful, shifty, spiv-like boy or girl

BANKER   A confident boy or girl; very worldly

BEAVER   An outsider; a boy with a harelip which is not a comedy device within the play but a terrible handicap

BONKERS   A boy or girl with excessive energy

BALACLAVA   A boy or girl whose mother is keen on knitting; always in a balaclava and often in Hovis jumpers as well

BOOTS   A boy or girl in boots far too big for them

BRAINS   A grammar school boy or girl

BARRISTER   A boy or girl of a sly barrack-room lawyer disposition

BAKER   A German Jewish refugee trying desperately to be one of the 'B's; he speaks with a German accent

THE NARRATORS   They have an unearthly quality – they could be victims of an earlier air raid watching this tragedy unfold; they should be costumed in the same period as the 'B's but their clothes are more ragged and almost white from brick dust, as is their hair and skin

VOICE OF MR HENDERSON   A school caretaker who keeps an eye on the allotments

ACT ONE

SCENE 1 • THE DIG

House lights down. Blackout. The sounds of bombs dropping followed by the all-clear siren are heard. Lights come up slowly on a bomb site. This was previously a terrace of houses but is now mostly rubble. It is roped off and on the rope are the signs 'No Looting' and 'Danger, Unexploded Bombs'.

Bellman appears in shadow from the back of the set and looks furtively down from the crest of the rubble to see if the coast is clear. Deciding it is, he slowly rings a handbell. Slowly, and with great purpose, more kids appear with him and swarm down the rubble. From down the road a large handmade barrow appears. It is pulled from the front by a rope and its overlong handles are supported by Bonkers and Barmy. In the barrow are broken and clumsily repaired garden tools, plus Beryl poling the barrow along. The barrow stops centre stage.

BELLMAN   Just the place for a Snark!

The Narrators appear.

NARRATOR 1   . . . the Bellman cried,
                    As he landed his crew with care;
                    Supporting each man on the top of the tide
                    By a finger entwined in his hair.

BELLMAN   Just the place for a snark!

NARRATOR 2   I have said it twice:
                    That alone should encourage the crew.

BELLMAN   Just the place for a snark!

NARRATOR 1   I have said it thrice.

BELLMAN   What I tell you three times is true.

NARRATOR 2   The crew was complete: it included a Boots –
                    A marker of Bonnets and Hoods –
                    A Barrister, brought to arrange their disputes –
                    And a Broker, to value their goods.

NARRATOR 1   A Billiard-marker, whose skill was immense,
                    Might perhaps have won more than his share –
                    But a Banker, engaged at enormous expense,
                    Had the whole of their cash in his care.

1

*The **Narrators** disappear.*

BELLMAN	Barmy, Bonkers, watch for the bobbies. Blagger, Brains, Boxer, start us a blaze. The rest of you bleeders burrow for bootle And bossy-boots Beryl build us a bog.
BERYL	Charming.
BELLMAN	It's important war work, Beryl. You know what happens when the 'B's do their business where they want. You reach in a hole, think you've found a banana and ugh . . .
BERYL	There aren't any bananas, not for the duration.
BARMY	(*sings*) There'll be bananas over The white cliffs of Dover Tomorrow just you wait and see.
BONKERS	(*sings*) There'll be pink and wobblies And packets of toffees Tomorrow when the world is free.
BARMY AND BONKERS	(*sing*) And Bossy Boots Beryl will sleep On her own little perch again.

They make chicken noises.

ALL EXCEPT BERYL	(*sing*) There'll be lard and dripping And at Christmas there'll be chicken Tomorrow when our Dads come home.
BARMY	I'm going to write to my Dad and tell him to bring me home a banana. He's in the jungle, you know. Burma.
BERYL	I thought last week you said he was in the desert.
BARMY	No – jungle.
BERYL	You did! You said the desert.

Baker, *who has been hovering out of things, has drifted over.* **Baker** *is overdressed in six coats and jackets. He is wearing all the clothes he possesses. He approaches* **Bellman** *nervously.*

BAKER	Please – what shall I do?

There is a general groan.

BELLMAN	Hunt like the rest.
BAKER	Yes. (*He starts to go to hunt and then turns*) Hunt what?
BONKERS	Hunt what? Hear that!
BARMY	Don't you know?

Beryl *advances on* **Baker**. *During the following dialogue* **Bonkers**, **Barmy** *and* **Billiard Ball** *join her and surround* **Baker**.

BERYL	He's brainless. What are you doing with all those coats on again?
BAKER	My mother likes me to wear them.
BILLIARD	His Mum's loopy.
BELLMAN	That right? Is your Mum loopy?
BAKER	(*quietly*) No.
BERYL	Then why does she make you wear six coats?
BILLIARD	Yeah, why?

Baker *shakes his head and tries to walk away.* **Bellman** *pulls him back.*

BELLMAN	You – what's your name? What's his name?
BILLIARD	What's his name?
BONKERS	Pepper pots!
BARMY	Mustard gas!
BAKER	Brunstein.
BELLMAN	What?
BAKER	Brunstein.
BELLMAN	Eh, what? What did you say?
BERYL	He doesn't know his own name.
BONKERS	(*as if talking to an idiot*) Do . . . you . . . know . . . your . . . own . . . name?

Baker *shakes his head. The others scream with delight and then freeze.* **Bellman**, **Beryl**, **Bonkers**, **Barmy** *and* **Billiard Ball** *are around* **Baker**. *The other* **'B's** *are further upstage on the rubble. The* **Narrators** *appear.*

NARRATOR 1	There was one who was famed for the number of things

He forgot when he entered the ship:
His umbrella, his watch, all his jewels and rings,
And the clothes he had bought for the trip.

He had forty-two boxes, all carefully packed,
With his name painted clearly on each:
But, since he omitted to mention the fact,
They were all left behind on the beach.

NARRATOR 2	The loss of his clothes hardly mattered, because He had seven coats on when he came, With three pairs of boots – but the worst of it was, He had wholly forgotten his name.
NARRATOR 1	He would answer to "Hi!" or to any loud cry, Such as "Fry me!" or "Fritter my wig!" To "What-you-may-call-um!" or "What-was-his- name!" But especially "Thing-um-a-jig!"

At the end of the narration the **Narrators** *disappear. All unfreeze and continue as before as if there has been no freeze.*

BERYL	Thing-um-a-jig, why are you wearing all them coats?
BONKERS	I never had that many coats.
BARMY	I have.
BERYL	(*to* **Barmy**) Liar, liar, bum's on fire.
BONKERS	(*to* **Baker**) They all yours?
BAKER	Yes.
BERYL	You look really stupid.
BAKER	Yes.
BELLMAN	You agree with everything?
BAKER	Yes.
BILLIARD	Are you stupid? I said, are you stupid?
BAKER	Yes.

The kids all laugh.

BARMY	Have you got a stupid name?
BAKER	Yes.
BERYL	Is your Mum daft?

Baker *tries to walk away again but he is pulled back by* **Bellman**.

BERYL	I said, is your Mum daft?

Baker *nods.*

BELLMAN	Why's she daft?
BAKER	Yes.
BELLMAN	No, that don't make sense. Listen – you can't say yes to everything, can you?
BAKER	No.
BELLMAN	Am I right?
BAKER	Yes.
BELLMAN	Or am I wrong?
BAKER	No.
BILLIARD	Get rid of him, Bellman, he's stupid. Send him back.
BELLMAN	Can't do that. He's an ally.
BILLIARD	I never heard of a Jew army.
BONKERS	What use is he, I say?
BAKER	I can hunt – with the others?
BELLMAN	Hunt what?
BAKER	I don't know.

There is a general laugh.

BERYL	What's your Dad do?
BAKER	He's a chef.
BELLMAN	Right, you can be our cook.
BARMY	Can you cook bangers?
BAKER	Yes.
BONKERS	And spuds?
BAKER	Yes.
BILLIARD	And pease puddin'?
BAKER	Yes.
BERYL	Do you know what bangers, spuds and pease pudding are?

BAKER	No.
BELLMAN	What am I going to do with you, oh, what's-your-name?
BILLIARD	Bumble bee.
BELLMAN	No, it's not.
BERYL	No good asking him – he won't remember.
BELLMAN	I'll call him cook.
BERYL	Cook don't begin with 'B'. Can't have a 'C' in the 'B's.
BELLMAN	All right, I'll call him Baker. All right you – you're not what-you-may-call-it any more, you're Baker. That's your nickname, right?
BERYL	Who are you?
BAKER	Nickname.
ALL	No – Baker.
BAKER	Baker. I am Baker.

The **'B's** *freeze and* **Narrator 1** *appears.*

NARRATOR 1	He came as a Baker: but owned when too late – And it drove the poor Bellman half mad – He could only bake Bridecake – for which, I may state, No materials were to be had.

The **Narrator** *disappears. The* **'B's** *unfreeze.*

BELLMAN	I want a volunteer to put Baker through basic.
BARMY	Never volunteer – that's what my Dad says. Mind you, last time he did he won an M.C.
BERYL	They only give the Military Cross to officers.
BARMY	He is an officer.

The kids scoff. **Barmy** *is known as a liar. They continue to hunt through the rubble inspecting any finds. Baiting* **Barmy** *is something they do from habit and doesn't need all their attention.* **Barmy**, *however, defends himself passionately.*

BARMY	He is!

BONKERS	What is he now? Admiral Barmy?
BARMY	No – Sergeant!
BERYL	Sergeant isn't an officer.
BARMY	You didn't let me finish – he's a . . . Sergeant Captain.
BILLIARD	There ain't no such rank in the British Army.
BARMY	He ain't in the British Army – he's with the Poles – Polenskis Flying Column.
BELLMAN	They're in the desert.
BARMY	That's right.
BERYL	But you said your Dad was in Burma.
BARMY	It's a mission – a secret mission!
BONKERS	What do you know about it?
BARMY	I . . . I . . . I might be involved in it. I can't say any more even if you torture me!
BELLMAN	That's against the Geneva Convention.
BERYL	(*to* **Barmy**) I don't believe you.

Baker, *seeing* **Barmy** *as an outsider like himself, has sidled over.*

BAKER	I do – I believe you.
BARMY	(*to* **Baker**) Piss off!
BELLMAN	What are we going to do about this Baker? Who's going to teach him the ropes?
BARMY	Not me – might interfere with my parachute training. Whoops!
BERYL	Give him to Beaver.

There is general agreement with this and laughter.

BELLMAN	Beaver? Not a bad idea, sticking our two non-combatants together.
BERYL	Beaver! Beaver! Come here.
BELLMAN	At the double, Beaver.

Beaver *detaches himself from the others and comes down.*

BELLMAN	Beaver, take Baker here under your wing.

BILLIARD	Under your lip.

There is a general mocking laugh.

BELLMAN	He's going to do our cooking.
BAKER	What shall I cook?
BELLMAN	Wait for it Baker, I'm coming to that. Don't jump the gun. We have discipline in the 'B's. That's why we won't be beaten and your lot was. Right?
BAKER	Yes.
BELLMAN	All right, Beaver, carry on. Take him down the allotments. We'll have a vegetable stew for supper.

Baker *and* **Beaver** *leave with the wheelbarrow. Lights down. Spotlight on* **Narrator 1**. *The* **'B's** *freeze.*

NARRATOR 1	There was also a Beaver, that paced on the deck, Or would sit making lace in the bow: And had often (the Bellman said) saved them from wreck, Though none of the sailors knew how.

The **Narrator** *disappears and the* **'B's** *exit.*

SCENE 2 • THE ALLOTMENTS

Spotlight on **Baker** *standing, looking bemused. The rubble set is still behind him but he stands by a scarecrow. Also on stage are two free-standing signs. One reads 'Bilton Road Allotments – No Trespassing'. The other reads 'Dig For Victory'.* **Beaver** *scuttles up beside him and pulls him down.*

BAKER   Sorry, is there danger? I didn't know. (*There is a pause*) Do we have to wait here long? (*There is a pause*) What are we waiting for? (*There is a pause*) Why don't you talk? Cat got your tongue?

Beaver *suddenly attacks* **Baker** *and they roll around on the ground.* **Baker** *jumps up.*

BAKER   Get off me! What's the matter with you? Are you mad or something? (*He inspects himself*) Now you've torn my coat. My coat is torn! My mother will be furious. Aren't you even going to apologise? Can't you even say sorry?

When **Beaver** *speaks it is apparent he has a harelip.*

BEAVER   Sorry.

BAKER   (*not understanding*) Sorry?

BEAVER   Sorry. About your coat. All right?

BAKER   Yes.

BEAVER   Get down.

Baker *does so.*

BAKER   Yes.

BEAVER   You have to watch out for Henderson.

BAKER   Yes.

BEAVER   You know him?

BAKER	No.
BEAVER	He keeps an eye on the allotments. He'll box your ears if he catches you.
BAKER	(*anxiously*) Box my ears?
BEAVER	Yeah – he caught Barmy nicking cabbages and gave him a cauliflower . . .
BAKER	Gave him a cauliflower?
BEAVER	Cauliflower ear – you know.
BAKER	Yes. (*Attempting a joke*) It was lucky he didn't catch him stealing carrots!
BEAVER	(*puzzled*) Why?
BAKER	He might have given him a carrot nose!

Baker *enjoys his own joke until he realises that* **Beaver** *hasn't. There is a silence between them. Suddenly* **Baker** *groans.*

BEAVER	What's wrong?
BAKER	I've forgotten my nickname. I meant to write it down.
BEAVER	Baker.
BAKER	Baker. That's right. I am Baker. And you're Beaver. Is that your forename or your surname?
BEAVER	Nickname.
BAKER	Nickname?
BEAVER	'Cos of this. (*He indicates his harelip*) Look like a beaver, don't I?
BAKER	That's not nice.
BEAVER	Don't worry about me. Sticks and stones can break my bones but words can never hurt me.
BAKER	No, you're wrong. First the words, then the sticks, then the broken bones.
BEAVER	What're you talking about?
BAKER	When the words no longer hurt you, then they'll beat you. When you don't feel any more pain, then they'll kill you.
BEAVER	You're bonkers.
BAKER	No, Bonkers is bonkers, I am Baker!

They both laugh.

BAKER	Why are you all 'B's?
BEAVER	It's patriotic. The gang ain't really called the 'B's. 'B's is short for 'Britons'. We're the 'Britons'. But that's a bit of a mouthful so we call ourselves the 'B's. And you've got to be a 'B' to get in.

*They move forward surreptitiously and start miming pulling up vegetables and putting them into a sack that **Beaver** carries.*

BAKER	What are the 'B's doing? On the bombed houses? What are they hunting for?
BEAVER	Snark.
BAKER	Snark?
BEAVER	And boodle.
BAKER	Boodle?
BEAVER	And scoff.
BAKER	Scoff?
BEAVER	Scoff is food. Sometimes you find a hoard of tin stuff or wedding cake in a tin or bottles of beer or ruby wine. We all got drunk on ruby wine once.
BAKER	I would like to get drunk on ruby wine.
BEAVER	Ain't it against your religion?
BAKER	I don't think so – Papa drank wine.
BEAVER	Your Dad in the Forces? Overseas?
BAKER	I don't know – he didn't come here with us.
BEAVER	Why not?
BAKER	There was a problem. You see, my mother had everything packed, in boxes. Everything was in boxes. The people helping us said we had to go, just go, just leave everything, leave the boxes. 'Do you want to die for your sideboards?' they said. My mother wouldn't leave, she wouldn't leave the boxes. My father tried to persuade her. He said he would stay, arrange a vehicle, and load the boxes, follow us, we were to go ahead. My mother was finally persuaded, so we left him with the boxes – and he hasn't arrived yet. We

are still waiting for him and the boxes. (*He becomes still remembering this*)

BEAVER	(*trying to cheer him up*) Want to know what boodle is?
BAKER	I know, it's a dog. A French dog with a ridiculous haircut.
BEAVER	That's a poodle. I said boodle. Boodle is valuables, jewels, treasure!
BAKER	Do you find treasure in the wrecked houses?
BEAVER	Not half.
BAKER	What do you do with it?
BEAVER	The Banker sells it to Uncles.
BAKER	His uncles?
BEAVER	Not his uncles – Uncles. Uncles is a pawnbroker.
BAKER	Oh.
BEAVER	Do you want some treasure?
BAKER	Yes please.
BEAVER	Here, don't tell the others – we're supposed to share everything.

Beaver *hands an object to* **Baker**. **Baker** *inspects it*.

BAKER	What is it?
BEAVER	A glass eye. Mr Hodges' glass eye. I could have let you have his false teeth as well but Beryl saw me pick them up.
BAKER	You're giving it to me?
BEAVER	If you want it.
BAKER	I do, yes, yes.
BEAVER	It's treasure.
BAKER	I know.
BEAVER	Don't let the others see it.
BAKER	I won't. I must give you something in return. When my father gets here with the boxes I will give you something.
BEAVER	You got treasure in the boxes then?
BAKER	The boxes are full of treasure – jewels, crowns,

golden candlesticks, necklaces, Snarks of silver.

BEAVER   Snarks?

BAKER   Aren't Snarks treasure?

BEAVER   No – it's ammo – spent rounds, that sort of thing.
               Know what I mean?

Baker *shakes his head.*

BEAVER   You've seen an air raid?

BAKER   I've heard them.

BEAVER   Well, afterwards you can find bits of the bombs
               lying around, sometimes big bits. Once a gang –
               the other side of the council estate – found a
               whole bomb, a Snark. That's what we're after – a
               Snark.

The voice of **Mr Henderson** *is heard off stage.*

HENDERSON Oi, you two, what're you doing over there?

Baker *stands up and looks towards the voice.* **Beaver** *grabs him by the
arm and rushes him off. Lights down.*

SCENE 3 • THE DIG

Lights up on the dig. The **'B's**, *apart from* **Beaver** *and* **Baker**, *are still at work in the rubble but the work has slowed in pace.* **Beryl** *moves amongst the others, chivvying them along.* **Bellman** *clears from the front, working the hardest. There is a pile of 'goods' lying centre stage that they have cleared from the rubble. It is a curious collection of kettles, picture frames, chipped ornaments and garden tools. Some discovered objects are added to the pile but others are thrown back into the rubble.* **Banker** *is near the pile of goods and he cleans them as best he can with a huge hanky.* **Barmy** *is the worst at bringing over useless objects that have to be thrown back into the rubble.* **Beaver** *and* **Baker** *rush on breathless.*

BEAVER	(*by way of explanation*) Henderson . . .
BAKER	He would have packed our ears.
BEAVER	(*correcting* **Baker**) Boxed.
BELLMAN	Get anything?

Beaver *nods and tips out the sack. It is now full with real vegetables: turnips, carrots, cabbages and spuds.*

BELLMAN	(*calling*) Banker! (**Banker** *comes over*) Get anything for this lot do you reckon?
BANKER	I could take them to Sid the Spiv.
BILLIARD	Give them to a Yank for some gum.
BONKERS	(*chanting*) 'Got some gum, chum?'
BERYL	My Mum says that's begging. My Mum says there's three things wrong with the Yanks – they're overpaid, they're over here and they're over-interested in the ladies.
BARMY	Oversexed, that's what your Mum said.
BERYL	My Mum doesn't use words like that!
BARMY	She does when the pub's closed. I've heard her rolling home!
BERYL	You filthy liar! She's never been in a pub in her life.
BARMY	She did a wee down a drain one night – I saw her.

BERYL	I'll kill him!
BAKER	So did I, I saw her!

*Beryl has been trying to corner the mocking **Barmy**. **Baker** has been stupid enough to join in while he is in reach of **Beryl**. **Beryl** turns and punches him hard in the stomach. **Baker** collapses. **Beryl** chases **Barmy** off.*

BARMY	Beryl's Mum does it for cheese coupons! (*He exits*)
BERYL	I'll kill you. (*She exits*)

Baker *lies weeping on the ground. The others ignore him.*

BELLMAN	Take them to the Spiv then.
BANKER	What about our supper?
BELLMAN	Oh, right. Sort a bit of this veg out for him. (*He indicates **Baker***) Then get him to cook it.
BILLIARD	How much have we got saved now, Banker?

Banker *produces a money-box and shakes it. It sounds very full.*

BANKER	Difficult to say. When we can't get any more in it I'll get the key off Bellman and we'll open it and count the money.
BILLIARD	And have a share out.
BONKERS	What about him? (*He indicates **Baker***) He's only just joined. Will he get the same as the rest of us?
BELLMAN	No. A refugee can't expect an equal share of the spoils of victory. I mean, we're fighting this war for them. Let them be grateful for that I say.
BANKER	Hear, hear.
BEAVER	What if he's the one who finds the Snark? The ultimate weapon? Will he get equal shares then?
BANKER	Him? He couldn't find his own way home.
BEAVER	That's 'cos he ain't got one.

Beaver *goes over and squats by **Baker**. He doesn't comfort him in any way but by his presence. There is a sudden series of loud screams from **Barmy** which are heard from offstage.*

BILLIARD	She got him then?
BELLMAN	Sounds like it.

Barmy *runs on crying.*

BARMY	She's loony she is. She's a certifiable loony. I'm going home. I want me shovel.

Bellman *hands it to him.*

BARMY	I might not come here again!
BEAVER	Parachute training?
BARMY	Yeah! Unarmed combat. When I've learned unarmed combat I'm going to come back here and shoot her.
BILLIARD	You don't have guns in unarmed combat.
BARMY	Shut up. Oh, here she comes – I'm going to get you, bossy knickers! I've got a gang and we're going to get you on our way home from school. (*He runs off*)

Beryl *walks on grimy triumphant.*

BAKER	(*to* **Beryl**) Sorry.
BERYL	(*with menace*) Have you ever had a Chinese burn?

Baker *nods.*

BEAVER	(*whispering*) No.

Baker *shakes his head.*

BONKERS	Go on Beryl, give him a Chinese burn.
BERYL	Give me your wrist.

Baker *meekly does so.* **Beryl** *takes it and applies a Chinese burn.* **Baker** *shouts and screams. The others cheer except* **Beaver**.

BEAVER	Leave him alone, Beryl.
BERYL	Shut up, rabbit face.
BONKERS	(*sings*) 'Run rabbit, run rabbit, run, run, run.'

16

BEAVER	He didn't understand.
BERYL	Everyone knows better than to insult someone's mother.

*Beryl finishes with **Baker** and he drops to his knees crying and holding his wrist.*

BAKER	(*crying again*) I didn't – I didn't understand. You all insulted my mother.
BERYL	(*indignantly*) No, we didn't.
BAKER	You called her lappy.
BEAVER	Loopy.
BAKER	Yes.
BELLMAN	That wasn't insulting, that was trying to get the facts straight.

*Bellman holds **Baker** on the shoulder.*

BELLMAN	You weren't really insulted, were you?
BEAVER	Yes!
BAKER	(*quietly*) No.
BEAVER	(*in disgust*) Oh Jesus! Get up off your knees, Baker.
BERYL	It's you who's going to be on your knees, goofy.

*The **'B's** come down off the rubble to taunt **Beaver**. During the following dialogue they glance nervously upstage centre to where **Butcher** finally appears from.*

BANKER	Yeah, he doesn't know he's back yet.
BEAVER	Who's back?
BERYL	Back from being evacuated he is.
BEAVER	Who?
BILLIARD	I reckon they kicked him out. No one would want him billoted on them.
BEAVER	Who?
BERYL	Who would you most hate to see walking down that street?
BONKERS	Rejoining the 'B's.

BILLIARD	Taking up where he left off.
BANKER	Teaching you to button your lip.
BERYL	Who do you hate most in the world?
BEAVER	Butcher.
BELLMAN	He's back.

*The **Narrators** appear. During the narration the '**B's** turn in slow motion to where **Butcher** appears in silhouette upstage centre.*

NARRATOR 1 He came as a Butcher; but gravely declared,
      When the ship had been sailing a week,
      He could only kill Beavers. The Bellman looked
       scared,
      And was almost too frightened to speak.

NARRATOR 2 The Beaver, who happened to hear the remark,
      Protested, with tears in his eyes,
      That not even the rapture of hunting the Snark
      Could atone for that dismal surprise!

*An air raid siren is heard. The kids start to leave in a business-like manner. There is no panic. They silently slip past **Butcher** on their way home. Only **Beaver**, **Baker**, **Beryl** and **Bellman** are left facing **Butcher**. **Butcher** is bigger than the other '**B's**. Even in wartime austerity his clothes are more ragged than normal. He almost looks like a giant rat amongst the rubble. His movements are rat-like: long freezes followed by fast, dangerous action.*
 *Evacuation had postponed a leadership struggle between **Butcher** and **Bellman**. Now he has returned the struggle will begin. **Bellman** is tough but **Butcher** is hard.*

NARRATOR 1 He came as a Butcher; but gravely declared,
      When the ship had been sailing a week,
      He could only kill Beavers. The Bellman looked
       scared,
      And was almost too frightened to speak.

*Beaver tries to pass **Butcher** to get home but **Butcher** pushes him back.*

BUTCHER Beaver.

NARRATOR 2 But at length he explained, in a tremulous tone,
      There was only one Beaver on board;
      And that was a tame one he had of his own,
      Whose death would be deeply deplored.

The **Narrators** *disappear.*

BUTCHER	So you're still with us, Beaver?
BAKER	There's going to be an air raid.
BUTCHER	Millions die and a deformed cripple like you survives. I think you've got a cheek. A liberty. Living, when you'd be better off dead.
BAKER	It's only a speech impediment.

Butcher *takes in* **Baker** *for the first time.*

BUTCHER	What's this?
BELLMAN	Baker – he's new.
BERYL	He's a Jew.
BUTCHER	In the 'B's? In the 'Britons'?
BELLMAN	He can cook.
BUTCHER	And you'd eat it? It'd make me sick – like him. (*Indicating* **Beaver**) He's always turned my gut. From the first day at school – you know, new teachers, new everything. Didn't know if I was coming or going and they sat me next to him – a monster. I couldn't take my eyes off him. It was the most disgusting thing I'd ever seen. I puked up my milk because of him. I couldn't sleep that night, I thought I might catch it.
BAKER	It's not contagious.
BERYL	How do you know? It's bad luck, I know that. My Mum told me.

Bombs are heard falling a long way away.

BAKER	I can hear the bombs.
BELLMAN	He does no harm.
BUTCHER	He's unclean.
BEAVER	(*through gritted teeth*) I hate you, Butcher.
BUTCHER	What did you say? What did this thing say to me? Listen, Beaver, don't blow off through your mouth.

Beryl *laughs.*

BELLMAN	(*to* **Beryl**) Shut up.
BERYL	Charming.
BAKER	We should be going home! We should be down a shelter.
BUTCHER	(*to* **Beryl**) You're a girl guide, prepared for any emergency. You got a needle and cotton?
BERYL	Yes.
BELLMAN	What you going to do, Butcher?
BUTCHER	Sew up his mouth.
BAKER	No! No! You can't! This is madness! Are you mad?
BUTCHER	Get out of my way or I'll do you, too.
BAKER	(*putting up his fists*) All right! Come on then!
BERYL	Stick! Stick a bombs!

There is a sudden pattern of bombs falling closer and closer to them.

BELLMAN	Run.
BEAVER	(*grabbing* **Baker**) Come on!
BERYL	Falling right on top of us!

There is a loud explosion. Blackout.

END OF ACT ONE

ACT TWO
SCENE 1 • THE DIG

There is even more destruction after the air raid. The 'No Looting' sign is smashed in two and the pieces lie on opposite sides of the rubble. The rope has been buried by fresh rubble and only emerges at the surface in places. Brick dust floats in the air. In the distance emergency service bells are heard ringing occasionally. The **'B's** *arrive in an excited manner but instead of setting to work immediately they group together centre stage.* **Boots** *strides on.*

BOOTS	You heard about Beryl?
BALACLAVA	Yes. Eh, Bellman, is it true about Beryl?
BELLMAN	Might be – might not.
BOOTS	There's Banker. Oi, Banker! Is it true?
BANKER	Might be.
BOOTS	Come on, did she?
BALACLAVA	How much is it worth?
BOOTS	Was it gold?
BANKER	Keep your voices down!
BELLMAN	That's right, don't tell the world.
BONKERS	Yeah, be like Dad . . .
BILLIARD	. . . Keep Mum.
BALACLAVA	But I want to know . . .

Beryl *appears unnoticed by the others. She watches and waits for her moment. This is her big day and she preens herself.*

BANKER	All right, shut up. Bellman?
BELLMAN	All right – but keep your traps shut. We don't want the rozzers after us.
BANKER	Well, it weren't gold or silver.
BERYL	I'll tell them. It was my find. (*She crosses to centre stage*)
BELLMAN	Fair enough.

BERYL	Well, yesterday was Saturday.
BARMY	(*sarcastic*) Oh yeah.
BERYL	I'm not telling if he's here.
BELLMAN	Clear off, Barmy.
ALL EXCEPT BELLMAN	Yeah, go on, shove off.
BARMY	I've got a right! I'm a 'B'!
BRAINS	I thought you were going off for parachute training?
BOXER	Unarmed combat?
BARMY	I'm awaiting my travel documents.
BRAINS	Are you? Oh, that's what he must have meant.
BARMY	Who?
BRAINS	The paratrooper I bumped into outside your house.
BARMY	Paratrooper? Outside my house?
BRAINS	Yeah, just for a moment I think he thought I was you, and he let slip more than he should have.
BARMY	What are you talking about?
BRAINS	Well, when he realised his mistake there was no point in holding anything back – so he told me . . .
BARMY	Told you what?
BRAINS	He wants you. Now. In Scotland. And take some flippers.
BARMY	Now? Scotland? I ain't got any flippers!
BELLMAN	Well, you can't hang about. Run and tell him.
BRAINS	In Scotland.
BARMY	I can't run to bleeding Scotland, can I?
BRAINS	It's an initiative test.
BELLMAN	Come on, Barmy, don't let the 'B's down. On your way.
BARMY	He's lying!
BARRISTER	But Brains's story holds out your story. I mean, if he's lying maybe so are you?
BRAINS	Am I lying, Barmy?

BARMY	(*struggling*) No – no!
BELLMAN	Well, off you go then.

With ill grace, **Barmy** *trots off.*

BOXER	Good luck in Scotland, Barmy!
BLAGGER	Don't forget the flippers!
BELLMAN	(*to* **Beryl**) Right, you've got five minutes before he makes an excuse and comes back.

Impatiently **Beryl** *beckons the others round her.* **Banker** *gives her an old chair from the rubble which she stands on.*

BERYL	Well, yesterday was Saturday and Saturday mornings I help me Mum on her milk round. She does the Medway Estate, all round there. Well, she gives me half a pint for old Mrs Beavis – she don't have a pint any more since her Billy went down with the Hood. Her house is an old'un, on its own in a creepy big garden . . .
BOXER	We've been scrumping there . . .
BERYL	That's right. It's dead early in the morning, right. And the air's full of that air raid smell if you know what I mean. Brick dust, burnt things. Not fresh like a morning should be. Anyway I come out of her bushes and there ain't no house . . .
BARRISTER	What do you mean – no house?
BERYL	It's gone, blown up. I mean, like normally there's a pile of bricks and things but this must have been a direct hit – just a ruddy big hole in the ground!
BELLMAN	No firemen?
BERYL	No one. I don't think anyone knew. It was a heavy raid the night before.

The others agree.

BALACLAVA	Our cat ain't come back yet.
BOOTS	A stick of bombs got within four doors of us.
BANKER	My Mum's talking about evacuation again. I

said, 'Mum, I run away before and I'll do it again.'

BERYL Well, I don't think anyone clocked Mrs Beavis had been blown up.

BOOTS What did you do?

BERYL I was going to run and tell Mum – but first I thought – I thought I may as well drink her milk. So I did. Well, having drunk her milk I wondered what else she might have.

BONKERS She didn't have anything except a great big hole in the ground.

BERYL Listen. When I looked I saw it wasn't a hole – it was her cellars. The bomb had blown her house clear away and the hole in the ground was her cellars, so I thought I'd go down and have a look see.

BARRISTER How?

BERYL Down the stone steps past her coal hole.

BANKER Hey, what happened to her coal?

BERYL My Mum had that – later. So I looked round. First of all I thought there was nothing.

Barmy's *voice is heard off stage.*

BARMY Thanks, Corporal, for putting me in the picture. Yeah, he got it a bit wrong – yeah, he said today. Of course not, no, next week then? I'll be there.

BARMY (*entering*) Oi Brains, wrong about the time, right about the flippers.

BRAINS Did you see him? The paratrooper?

BARMY Yeah.

BRAINS Big fellow, blonde with a 'tache?

BARMY That's right.

BRAINS Funny – para I spoke to was a bald midget.

BARMY (*thrown*) No! What? You're right! Now I come to think about it . . .

BELLMAN Barmy! Shut up! Stay there!

BARMY Don't you want to know what sort of deep sea

	diving I need those flippers for?
BRAINS	Flippers? Oh God, Barmy, I just remembered he didn't say flippers – he said bicycle clips.
BARMY	(*sinking fast*) Oh yeah, bicycle clips – that's right.
BRAINS	Great, Barmy! Tell us what sort of deep sea diving it is that you need bicycle clips for?
BARMY	(*momentarily nonplussed*) Well . . . you're not going to credit this but . . . (*brainwave*) the Boffins have made a breakthrough!
BELLMAN	I said shut it, Barmy, and don't move.
BARMY	I can't tell you anyway. It's top secret.
BELLMAN	Shut it!
BARMY	Yeah.
BELLMAN	Right.
BARMY	. . . but in a funny way I pity those sharks.
BELLMAN	(*furious*) Barmy, if you open your mouth once more, or move an inch, I'll hit you with this brick.

Barmy *indicates that his lips are sealed and that he accepts* **Bellman's** *orders to stay where he is as if it is a place of honour – a forward position in action.*

BERYL	(*whispering to exclude* **Barmy**) Well, I thought I was wasting my time when, hello, I sees a couple of milk bottles on a shelf. Some people do that – don't realise they're only buying the milk and the bottles is only lent – so I think I might as well take them when I sees they ain't empty. I thought it was mould – some people put their milk bottles out without rinsing them – Barmy's Mum does . . .
BARMY	(*from his great distance*) No, she doesn't!
BERYL	I thought so . . . (*she moves her crowd as far from* **Barmy** *as possible*) but it don't sniff like mould so I drop one to break it – to see what was inside . . .
BOOTS	What was it?
BERYL	Fivers. Fivers, five pound notes.

BALACLAVA	Five pound notes?
BERYL	Great big white ones, big like a man's hanky. Ten of them and ten in the other bottle.
BILLIARD	That's a hundred quid, that's all the money in the world.
BANKER	Nearly.
BOOTS	I reckon that was her burying money.
BOXER	A hundred quid? It don't take a hundred quid. She probably did a penny a week policy with the Provvy, like everyone else.
BOOTS	But supposing it was her burying money.
BERYL	'Course it wasn't. Anyway, so what? She don't need a grave, do she? Not if she's blown up.
BALACLAVA	What happened?
BERYL	I heard me Mum calling so I hid the fivers.
BOOTS	Where?
BERYL	Down me knickers.
BARMY	Errr!
BOOTS	Where are they now?
BANKER	(*raising money-box*) In here.
BOOTS	Let's have a look!
BANKER	No! I've seen this sort of thing before. Men running wild at the sight of golden treasure.
BILLIARD	What are we going to do with it?
BELLMAN	I don't know – share it, I suppose.
BOOTS	When?
BELLMAN	(*to* **Banker**) When?
BANKER	Soon.
BERYL	Anyway, it's five to ten.
BELLMAN	Yeah. Right, back to work. Get down to the cellars, that's the best place to look. Boxer, stay with me. And you, Blagger.
BONKERS	What time's he coming?
BLAGGER	Where's Beaver and Baker?
BELLMAN	I've got them out of the way – given them the day off to go fishing.

BERYL	Here he is.
BELLMAN	(*to* **Beryl**) You'd better go.
BERYL	Why? I'm a better fighter than this lot. (*She indicates* **Boxer** *and* **Blagger**)

Butcher *enters.*

BUTCHER	You wanted to see me, Bellman?
BELLMAN	Yeah. I want you to leave Beaver alone.
BUTCHER	What I do to Beaver is none of your business.
BELLMAN	I'm Bellman. (*He squares up to* **Butcher**)
BUTCHER	Come on then! I'm ready. About time we had the third.
BELLMAN	You've given me a pasting and I've given you one. Leave it like that.
BUTCHER	Scared I might win?
BELLMAN	Yeah, scared you might ruin the 'B's. You're not a Bellman you're a Butcher.
BERYL	(*to the others*) That's right, isn't it?

The others are a bit reluctant to commit themselves being face to face with **Butcher**.

BERYL	I said, isn't it?

The others say 'yeah' and move behind **Bellman**.

BELLMAN	So you can beat me but you'll not get the 'B's. No one wants you to be Bellman. So if I say leave Beaver alone – leave him alone, right?
BUTCHER	(*senses he has lost this round*) Just keep him out of my way! (*He strides off*)

The others go away leaving **Bellman** *and* **Beryl**.

BELLMAN	Thanks.
BERYL	He'll beat you next time.

The **Narrators** *appear.*

NARRATOR 1	It was strongly advised that the Butcher should be

Conveyed in a separate ship:
But the Bellman declared that would never agree
With the plans he had made for the trip.

NARRATOR 2   The Beaver's best course was, no doubt, to procure
A second-hand dagger-proof coat –
So the Baker advised it – and next, to insure
Its life in some Office of note.

Lights down.

SCENE 2 • THE CANAL

Baker and **Beaver** *are sitting by the bank with their bare feet in the water.* **Beaver** *has a line into the water.* **Baker** *kicks his feet in the water.*

BEAVER	Don't do that, you'll scare the fish.
BAKER	Sorry – do you want to swim later?
BEAVER	Can't swim. Anyway you get the lurgy if you swim in the cut. Too many dead dogs in it.

Baker *takes this in and quietly pulls his feet out and dries them on one of his coats.*

BEAVER	Mum still make you wear the coats?
BAKER	No. She doesn't remember. She doesn't remember anything very much. Any more.
BEAVER	Worried about your Dad?
BAKER	(*bitterly*) Worried about the boxes.
BEAVER	Why do you wear the coats then?
BAKER	Getting like her perhaps.

They laugh. There is a pause. It is pleasant by the water and the two are now good enough friends to sit in silence.

BAKER	*Are* there any fish in this canal?
BEAVER	So the rumour goes.
BAKER	Do you eat them?
BEAVER	Ugh.
BAKER	Why do you catch them?

Beaver *suddenly asks the question that has been on his mind since the incident with* **Butcher**.

BEAVER	Why did you stick up for me – with Butcher? He'd have done you as well.
BAKER	Yes.
BEAVER	Oh, don't go back to saying yes to everything.

BAKER	No.
BEAVER	Stop it!
BAKER	Yeah . . . right.
BEAVER	Well?
BAKER	Look, are you an orthodox Christian?
BEAVER	I don't know what you're talking about.
BAKER	Are you a Christian?
BEAVER	Yes.
BAKER	Do you go to church every week?
BEAVER	No – we never go.
BAKER	So you are an unorthodox Christian.
BEAVER	We go for christenings, marriages and funerals.
BAKER	My family's the same. Unorthodox. Some things we observe, one thing especially . . .
BEAVER	Yeah?
BAKER	For boys – when we are babies – an operation.
BEAVER	In church? With hymns?
BAKER	No, no. (*He whispers in* **Beaver's** *ear*)
BAKER	Ugh! That's horrible, it makes me feel funny. Don't it hurt?
BAKER	I don't remember.
BEAVER	What do they do with it? After?
BAKER	What?
BEAVER	The bit they've pruned?
BAKER	I don't know – but look, that's not the point. You see, down there we look different.
BEAVER	Show me.
BAKER	No! That's not what I'm trying to say. Look, I went to a non-Jewish school and when I started school, the first day, the very first day – well, you remember how that felt? Well, in the playtime all the boys were sent to the boys' lavatories and we stood in a line. And, well, there's not much to do facing a wall, waiting for the wee wee to come so, you know, you sort of look around, you glance down at your partners' – well, you know. Well, the boy next to me must have glanced at mine . . .
BEAVER	And?
BAKER	I think he must have been related to Butcher. He

went berserk. Wet himself! Was sick on his shoes. He pointed at me with a trembling finger and said 'He's doing it through an acorn.'

They laugh.

BAKER   Boys like him – and Butcher – they have something missing themselves, in their heads.

BEAVER   I wish you'd sat next to me first day at school.

BAKER   I wish you'd stood next to me in the lavatories.

They laugh. Suddenly **Beaver** *gets excited and starts hauling in the line. Up comes an improvised 1940s fishing trawl. In the net is a fish.*

BAKER   You did it! You caught a fish!

BEAVER   Quick, get the jam jar! Put some water in it!

BAKER   You caught a fish! I'll give you a prize, a piece of treasure from the boxes!

The **Narrators** *appear.*

NARRATOR 1   This the Banker suggested, and offered for hire
                 (On moderate terms), or for sale,
                 Two excellent Policies, one Against Fire
                 and one Against Damage From Hail.

NARRATOR 2   Yet still, ever after that sorrowful day,
                 Whenever the Butcher was by,
                 The Beaver kept looking the opposite way,
                 And appeared unaccountably shy.

The **Narrators** *disappear. Lights down.*

SCENE 3 • THE DIG

Lights up on the dig. The whole gang is eating soup. There is a dusk feeling about the lighting. **Bellman** *stands up and addresses the gang.*

    Butcher *is sitting in an old deckchair salvaged from the rubble. He is eating his soup carefully as someone who has known hunger. He doesn't slop it with hasty gulping. He eats with dreadful concentration. His soup lasts longer than anyone else's. He alone has seconds which* **Baker** *serves him nervously. Only when he has finished eating will* **Butcher** *pay any attention to what's going on around him.*

BELLMAN	There's a lot of loose talk going on about not needing to find a Snark now we're rich.

Banker *stands.*

BANKER	Don't get us wrong, Bellman – nothing to do with the treasure, I've just never known what we needed a Snark for.
BARRISTER	Me, too.
BELLMAN	Because if we had a Snark no one could push us around. The Council gang's got some ammo, the Abbey Estate's got dud ack ack but no one ain't got a Snark.
BARRISTER	That's because they go off, Bellman. You know, with a bang.
BELLMAN	Not all explosives go off. My uncle bought a Mills bomb home from the last war. My aunty keeps it on her mantlepiece.
BARRISTER	You couldn't keep a landmine on your mantlepiece.
BELLMAN	I don't want it as an ornament. I want it as a warning. Anyone give us any trouble and 'kerboom'!!
BANKER	But we haven't got a plane to drop it from.
BARRISTER	I mean, even if you found an unexploded Snark how would you use it against the Council gang?
BELLMAN	I've thought that out. You see we fight a pitch

	battle but, on a secret signal, pretend to be beaten and run away. They chase us and we lead them into the ambush – we lead them to where we've hidden the Snark. We all jump in to slip trenches and then . . .
BARMY	(*excited*) Yeah?
BELLMAN	A volunteer hits the Snark with a hammer!
BARMY	Sounds logical.
BARRISTER	Of course, it's a suicide mission.
BELLMAN	As I said – it's a job for a volunteer.

All the boys volunteer themselves with grim faces and deep voices e.g. 'I'll do it', 'Count on me', 'Put me down'. They freeze in heroic poses as the **Narrators** *appear.*

NARRATOR 1	This was charming, no doubt: but they shortly found out That the Captain they trusted so well Had only one notion for crossing the ocean, And that was to tingle his bell.
NARRATOR 2	He was thoughtful and grave – but the orders he gave Were enough to bewilder a crew. When he cried "Steer to starboard, but keep her head larboard!" What on earth was the helmsman to do?

The **Narrators** *disappear. The action continues.* **Butcher** *goes for his seconds of soup at this point.*

BANKER	I can see the point of a Snark now. It's just that I don't think we're very likely to find one. Whereas we've been quite lucky with the looting . . .
BELLMAN	(*correcting him*) Living off the land.
BANKER	Living off the land. Shouldn't we be doing more of that? I mean, why wait for the houses to be blown up?
BELLMAN	What do you mean?
BANKER	We could get in them while the people are down in the air raid shelter. In and out through the back door or coal hole. It'd save hours of digging

	through the rubble if we did the houses before they were blown up.
BELLMAN	But that's thieving.
BANKER	So's looting.
BELLMAN	But the sort of stuff we take nobody'd want.
BARRISTER	What, like a hundred pounds in fivers?
BERYL	Finders keepers. She had no one to leave it to.
BARRISTER	How do we know? Maybe she's got a long lost relative.
BELLMAN	You're saying Beryl should have handed it in?
BANKER	No! No! What Barrister is saying is it's dog eat dog. We're doing all right out of this war – made a fair bit – but we could make more if we stopped wasting our time looking for a Snark.
BELLMAN	Listen! The 'B's only began turning over the bomb sites to find a Snark – the ruby wine, the fivers, they were an accident. I reckon if people are going to get greedy we should go back to just hunting a Snark and blow the treasure.
BERYL	But what about the treasure we've already found?
BELLMAN	Donate it – to the war effort. We could have a plane or a destroyer named after us – HMS Britons.

There is general interest in this idea.

BANKER	Let's not be hasty.
BARRISTER	And remember the danger. My uncle told me the Germans dropped Boojums.
BELLMAN	What's he mean?
BARRISTER	A Boojum is a Snark with a delayed detonator.
BELLMAN	And what's the point of that?
BARRISTER	It's to kill bomb disposal teams. They think it's a dud and start to defuse it and 'Boojum'!!
BELLMAN	Make a note of that, everyone.
BAKER	A Boojum – I didn't know there was danger. I thought we were looking for duds.

The action freezes as the **Narrators** *appear.*

NARRATOR 1 "But oh, beamish nephew, beware of the day,
If your Snark be a Boojum! For then
You will softly and suddenly vanish away,
And never be met with again!"

NARRATOR 2 But if ever I meet with a Boojum that day,
In a moment (of this I am sure)
I shall softly and suddenly vanish away –
and the notion I cannot endure!

The **Narrators** *disappear. The action continues.*

BERYL But what are we going to do about the treasure?

BELLMAN I don't know.

BALACLAVA Couldn't we at least count it? I haven't even seen it.

BELLMAN Yeah, we'll count it.

BANKER Now? It's getting late.

BELLMAN We'll count it tomorrow. We'll count it out tomorrow and then decide what to do with it.

The air raid siren begins.

BILLIARD They're early tonight.

BEAVER I haven't finished my soup.

BUTCHER Yeah, as soon as he takes a sip it spills out again.

The kids are going home quickly. **Banker** *and* **Barrister** *go into a hurried conference together.* **Baker** *gets too close to their whispering and they push him away.*

BEAVER (*to* **Baker**) Come on – air raid.

BUTCHER That's right – run home hand in hand like little girls.

BAKER There are going to be bombs.

BUTCHER Don't worry me. I like air raids. I like to sit out in them, in a deckchair – like it's summer and I'm on the beach. I love 'em better than fireworks. Go on home then, if you're going . . .

*There's something in **Butcher's** bravado that makes **Beaver** suspicious.*

BEAVER	No.
BAKER	What?
BEAVER	(*airily*) No, I like them as well. I might carry on hunting. I might find a fresh one.
BUTCHER	(*alarmed*) What? Aren't you going home?
BEAVER	No, not if you're not. You sit in your deckchair. I won't bother you.
BAKER	You're mad.
BEAVER	(*to* **Baker**) Go home. Your mother'll be worried.
BAKER	(*shakes his head*) She's in hospital. I'll stay.

The distant sound of bombs dropping is heard.

BUTCHER	What! You can't! You're both bloody mental! Go home before we're blown to bits!
BEAVER	We'll be all right, Butcher. We won't disturb you. You settle down in the deckchair and watch the display.

*Unwilling **Butcher** sits in the chair and **Banker** comes over to **Baker**.*

BANKER	Make yourself useful. Take the money-box. (*He hands the money-box to* **Baker**)
BAKER	Me? Why?
BANKER	Bellman wants it first thing. I can't make it – got to go to my nephew's christening. So don't lose it, eh? Take it home now.

There is a sudden nearer sound of bombs going off.

BANKER	Cripes, that was close! I'm off!
BAKER	(*to* **Beaver**) What am I supposed to do with this?
BEAVER	Take it home – quick!

Baker *sets off home.*

BEAVER	(*to* **Butcher**) I won't disturb you there, will I?

Butcher *tightly shakes his head but doesn't speak as more bombs are* *heard falling closer and closer.* **Beaver** *sifts through the rubble. The raid builds up in intensity.* **Butcher** *sits trapped centre stage in a deckchair as the bombs seem to get closer to him personally. He starts to cry quietly and rocks in misery.* **Beaver** *is behind the deckchair and is unaware of this. Suddenly there is quiet apart from the sound of a bomber approaching. Both boys listen intently to this. The engine noise gets closer and when it seems to be just overhead it cuts out. A whistle is heard as the bombs fall down. There is an almighty explosion. As the dust clears the bombs start to fall again and* **Butcher** *is standing having hysterics.* **Beaver** *rushes to him.*

BEAVER   What's up? Are you hit?!

Butcher *falls on the floor at* **Beaver's** *feet and hugs* **Beaver's** *knees while he sobs.* **Beaver** *is at a loss. Then he gently strokes* **Butcher's** *hair.*

BEAVER   It's all right – it's all right me old mate. I'm here, I'm here.

Lights down. Blackout.

SCENE 4 • THE DIG

Lights up on the following morning. Smoke drifts around as if the set is smouldering. The deckchair is a wreck. **Butcher** *is holding it up to show all the other* **'B's**.

BUTCHER   Well, I was sitting in this chair and bombs were falling all around. Me old mate Beaver was working away just north of me and I thought, things are getting a bit hot Butcher boy, time you wasn't here. So I called to Beaver and we beetled off to his place. I spent the night there, in his Dad's bed – his Dad's on the convoys. In the morning we had porridge. My Mum never bothers with me – bit of fried bread if I'm lucky. I'm going round for tea on Sunday. She does jam – her own jam, you know, made out of real things that grow.

BAKER   (*quietly to* **Beaver**) Can I come?

BEAVER   (*awkwardly*) I don't know.

The **Narrators** *appear. The action freezes.*

NARRATOR 1   Such friends, as the Beaver and Butcher became,
Have seldom if ever been known;
In winter or summer, 'twas always the same –
You could never meet either alone.

NARRATOR 2   And when quarrels arose – as one frequently finds
Quarrels will, spite of every endeavour –
The song of the Jubjub recurred to their minds,
And cemented their friendship for ever!

The **Narrators** *disappear. The action continues.*

BERYL   Quiet!

The talking stops. Out of the silence a creaking is heard coming closer.

BERYL   It's the telegram boy.

BOOTS	Don't let him turn down our street.
BERYL	He's in it already.

The cast watch an imaginary telegram boy cycle between them and the audience as if he is cycling down their street. Some faces show relief as he obviously passes their house. Then the creaking stops. In their own time, all turn and look with downcast eyes towards **Brains** *who is frozen to the spot. Finally . . .*

BERYL	Brains – your house.
BRAINS	My house – no! (*He runs down and off*)
BELLMAN	(*to* **Beryl**) Go with him – might just be notification of a wound.

Beryl *exits after* **Brains**.

BAKER	What – what happened?
BOOTS	The telegram boy.
BALACLAVA	I hate him.
BAKER	Why? What has he done?
BOOTS	He brings the telegrams. You know, about your Dad.
BALACLAVA	If something happens to him. You know, in battle.
BILLIARD	Missing. They say missing in action – believed killed.
BAKER	So Brains's father is . . .
BELLMAN	Maybe. We don't know.
BAKER	Will they send a telegram to me – one day?

The action freezes. **Narrator 1** *appears.*

NARRATOR 1	He thought of his childhood, left far far behind – That blissful and innocent state – The sound so exactly recalled to his mind A pencil that squeaks on a slate!

The **Narrator** *disappears. The action continues.*

BELLMAN	Here's Beryl, she's coming back. Well?

| BERYL | Missing, believed . . . (*mimes cutting throat*) |

They are all stunned at their friend's tragedy.

BARMY	I'm going to write to my father and tell him to kill a thousand of those so and so's! That'll cheer Brains up. I'll tell my Dad to take his submarine and . . .
BELLMAN	Barmy, for God's sake – everyone knows your Dad's in the nick! Everyone knows he's a villain – locked up on Dartmoor – so just shut up for once!
BARMY	Oh, I know that. I know you know that about him. I know that. But he ain't me real Dad. That's the truth, by the way – my Mum told me. So I must have a real Dad somewhere, mustn't I? Well, maybe he's got a submarine? Maybe he's in the jungle or desert. Well, (*desperate*) he might be, mightn't he?
BELLMAN	Maybe.
BARMY	Yeah, maybe. That's what I say. Maybe.
BELLMAN	Now let's get on. Where's Banker? Time for the count out.
BAKER	He's not coming. He's at his nephew's chiselling.
BEAVER	(*correcting*) Christening.
BAKER	I have the money-box.
BELLMAN	And I have the key. Right, put it down here and I'll open it.

Bellman *opens the box. There is immediate consternation. It is full of stones and bits of torn-up newspaper. The kids ad lib their anger. In a corner* **Barrister** *beckons to* **Banker** *who comes running on. As* **Banker** *passes they give each other a sly 'thumbs up' sign.*

BANKER	(*running on*) Sorry I'm late. Well, how much then?
BERYL	Nothing! It's been stolen! This box is full of torn paper and stones.
BANKER	Empty? Empty? (*He suddenly grabs* **Baker** *by his lapels*) You thief! What have you done with our money?

The others group round them.

BAKER	What? What? I haven't taken the money.
BARRISTER	Have you any grounds for this allegation, Banker?
BANKER	I certainly have, Barrister. This box was full of money when I gave it to him last night. Now it's empty. It stands to reason he's been at it.
BAKER	What about you? Maybe you gave me a box full of stones and paper.

Banker *goes for* **Baker**.

BANKER	I'll have him! He's calling me a thief!
BAKER	(*desperately*) You're calling me one.
BELLMAN	Look, are there any witnesses?
BEAVER	I saw Banker give Baker the money-box.
BELLMAN	And did he go straight home?
BEAVER	I think so.
BAKER	Yes!
BUTCHER	No! (*to* **Beaver**) Don't you remember – we saw him come creeping back again.
BAKER	No! I went straight home!
BELLMAN	Be quiet.
BERYL	Shut it!
BUTCHER	(*to* **Beaver**) You remember – he didn't see us. He squatted down just over there, didn't he?
BAKER	It's a lie!
BELLMAN	Go on.
BUTCHER	(*to* **Beaver**) What happened then?
BEAVER	I don't remember.
BUTCHER	Yes, you do. He got out a great bunch of keys.
BAKER	I don't have any keys!
BILLIARD	He's hidden them again.
BUTCHER	I said to Beaver, 'What's he up to?' and Beaver said, 'Counting his money, Jews always have money.' That's what you said, didn't you?

BELLMAN	(*to* **Beaver**) Well!?
BARRISTER	Well, Beaver?
BUTCHER	Well, Beaver? Tell the truth. You did say that, didn't you?

Beaver *stands silently, in agony. Finally, he's nearly one of the gang but the price is betraying* **Baker**. *He gives up the struggle and says what they want to hear.*

BEAVER	Yes.
BAKER	(*appalled at* **Beaver**) Liar, liar.
BARRISTER	Right, that's that. He's guilty!
BANKER	Too true!
BELLMAN	Hang on! I don't like it.

They all groan.

BERYL	What's wrong, Bellman? It's obvious. Even his friend won't lie to save him.
BUTCHER	I reckon Bellman's calling me a liar.
BELLMAN	It's not unknown for you to lie.
BUTCHER	Right, that does it!
BELLMAN	I warned you, Butcher. Now you've asked for it all right. (*He calls*) Boxer! Blagger! Over here.

The two named don't come but glance towards **Barrister** *who shakes his head.*

BELLMAN	Beryl?
BERYL	I told you. You wouldn't listen. Now you're going to lose . . .

Beryl *joins the others behind* **Butcher** *facing the lone* **Bellman**. **Butcher** *and* **Bellman** *square up and start to circle as the lights go down. Blackout. The* **'B's** *are heard shouting as if watching a fight. Silence follows.*

SCENE 5 • THE DIG

Lights up. **Baker** *is alone, digging. His digging has a frenzied, unnatural quality to it. It is more like someone looking for a lost loved one under the bricks.* **Beaver** *enters and stops awkwardly when he sees* **Baker**. *He decides he hasn't seen him and carries on. Then he stops himself and turns round.*

BEAVER	I thought you'd gone.
BAKER	(*continuing to hunt*) No.
BEAVER	Someone said you had.
BAKER	No.
BEAVER	Beryl said you'd gone to a home. That your Mum's broken down.
BAKER	(*correcting him*) *Had* a breakdown. Can't you even speak your own language?

There is a long pause.

BEAVER	Still here then? (**Baker** *doesn't answer*) Butcher's Bellman now.
BAKER	I'm not interested.
BEAVER	You should be. I told Butcher not to let them get you – over the money. He listens to me.
BAKER	(*sarcastically*) Thank you.
BEAVER	It was the least . . . (*He fades out*) What are you doing?
BAKER	Hunting.
BEAVER	What for? A Snark? We don't bother any more.
BAKER	I do.
BEAVER	Why?
BAKER	I want a Snark.
BEAVER	What for?
BAKER	For protection.
BEAVER	But Banker was right. You can't shoot it, you

can't drop it, what good is it?

BAKER   No – Bellman was right. I'll sit by it, with a hammer, with my boxes, and if anyone comes near . . .

BEAVER   That's daft – it's not worth it.

BAKER   Yes, it is. For me.

There is another long pause.

BEAVER   Mum's made some more jam.

BAKER   (*with great deliberation*) Please – leave me alone.

BEAVER   Have you run away?

BAKER   What from?

BEAVER   The home?

BAKER   It's not a home.

BEAVER   Where will you live?

BAKER   Here, there.

BEAVER   But how will your Dad find you – when he comes with the boxes?

Baker *suddenly goes frantic and points.* **Beaver** *is bewildered.*

BAKER   Look! Look! Can't you see?!

BEAVER   What?

BAKER   Coming down the road! Creak! Creak! It's the boy on the bike. Go past my house! Go past my house! But he's stopping, he's coming over the rubble, towards me. There is a problem, I can't remember my name . . . but it's for me – a paper. Will Beryl steal it from me? I don't think so – I will open it. (*He becomes very quiet, very natural*) It's, it's my father – he's missing, believed dead. Papa is dead.

BEAVER   You don't know that. He might turn up with the boxes of treasure!

BAKER   And when I open the boxes, the treasure will have turned to paper and stones.

BEAVER   I'm sorry.

BAKER   I don't blame you.

BEAVER	It's just – Butcher – I need him.
BAKER	I know. I need the Snark.
BEAVER	Yeah, that's right.
BAKER	No one cheeks you if you've got a Butcher or a Snark.
BEAVER	I'll help you.
BAKER	There's no need.
BEAVER	Yeah. It's only fair. I've got Butcher – you've got to have a Snark.

Beaver *starts to root around in the rubble.*

BAKER	I've looked over there.
BEAVER	What about the top?
BAKER	No.
BEAVER	We'll start there.

Baker *seems to burrow down into the rubble out of sight. He has formed a chain with* **Beaver** *who is half-way up the rubble. The lights start to fade.* **Beaver** *receives the bricks and domestic clutter that* **Baker** *hands up to him as well as each of* **Baker's** *six coats at regular intervals. He lays these carefully on the rubble. The drone of bombers passing overhead can be heard. When the light has almost gone and the last coat has been positioned,* **Baker's** *voice is heard.*

BAKER	Here! It's here! A Snark!

The lights go down. Blackout. The lights come up as the **'B's**, *led by* **Beaver***, run on and group at the bottom of the rubble.* **Baker** *has disappeared from view.*

BEAVER	He's done it! He's found one! He's found a Snark.
BERYL	A whole one?
BEAVER	We think so. He needs help to uncover it.
BELLMAN	I never thought we'd find one.
BEAVER	He did. He never gave up. He knew it – he wasn't even surprised when we uncovered the fin.
BARMY	Eh up, Baker! Where are you?

Baker *appears on top of the rubble and freezes in triumph above the* **'B's**

NARRATOR 1   "It's a Snark!" was the sound that first came to
their ears,
And seemed almost too good to be true.
Then followed a torrent of laughter and cheers:
Then the ominous words "It's a Boo——"

NARRATOR 2   Then, silence. Some fancied they heard in the air
A weary and wandering sigh
That sounded like "–jum!" but the others declare
It was only a breeze that went by.

The **Narrators** *disappear. The action continues.*

BAKER   Get away!! Go! Get away!!

BEAVER   (*confused and hurt at* **Baker's** *words*) They've
come to help, Baker.

BAKER   (*urgently*) You don't understand – it's started to
tick – it's a Boo . . .

There is a very loud explosion. As the earth begins to settle the **'B's** *search
the rubble without hope. They find* **Baker's** *coat but nothing else.
There is no dead body.* **Baker** *has just disappeared. They continue
hunting and discover the coats during the* **Narrators'** *speeches.
The light fades during the narration until there is only a spotlight on*
Narrator 2 *which fades out on the last line.*

NARRATOR 1   They hunted till darkness came on, but they found
Not a button, or feather, or mark,
By which they could tell that they stood on the
ground
Where the Baker had met with the Snark.

NARRATOR 2   In the midst of the word he was trying to say,
In the midst of his laughter and glee,
He had softly and suddenly vanished away –
For the Snark *was* a Boojum, you see.

END

THE HUNTING OF
THE SNARK BY LEWIS CARROLL

The story of Lewis Carroll's poem, *The Hunting of the Snark*, on which the play is based, tells of the strange and mysterious adventures of Bellman and his crew who set out in a boat to hunt for a Snark. As none of them has ever seen a Snark they have no idea what it is or what it looks like but the search gives the crew – Butcher, Beaver, Banker and the rest – a purpose for their journey. All of them, though, are hopelessly ill-prepared for their mission.

It is a long nonsense poem, written in ballad form, and is divided into eight sections. When you have read the play, you may find it fun to read the original poem. Try the edition produced by the artist Helen Oxenbury, published by William Heinemann Limited. Here are some of her illustrations of scenes and characters, as well as some extra verses from the poem.

THE LANDING

"Just the place for a Snark!" the Bellman cried,
  As he landed his crew with care;
Supporting each man on the top of the tide
  By a finger entwined in his hair.

"Just the place for a Snark! I have said it twice:
  That alone should encourage the crew.
Just the place for a Snark! I have said it thrice:
  What I tell you three times is true."

THE CREW

The crew was complete: it included a Boots –
  A maker of Bonnets and Hoods –
A Barrister, brought to arrange their disputes –
  And a Broker, to value their goods.

A Billiard-marker, whose skill was immense,
  Might perhaps have won more than his share
But a Banker, engaged at enormous expense,
  Had the whole of their cash in his care.

BEAVER

There was also a Beaver, that paced on the deck,
   Or would sit making lace in the bow:
And had often (the Bellman said) saved them from wreck,
   Though none of the sailors knew how.

BAKER

There was one who was famed for the number of things
   He forgot when he entered the ship:
His umbrella, his watch, all his jewels and rings,
   And the clothes he had bought for the trip.

He had forty-two boxes, all carefully packed,
   With his name painted clearly on each:
But, since they omitted to mention the fact,
   They were all left behind on the beach.

The loss of his clothes hardly mattered, because
   He had seven coats on when he came,
With three pair of boots – but the worst of it was,
   He had wholly forgotten his name.

BELLMAN

Bellman seems to be the only person who knows anything about Snarks.

"Come, listen, my men, while I tell you again
  The five unmistakable marks
By which you may know, wheresoever you go,
  The warranted genuine Snarks.

"Let us take them in order. The first is the taste,
  Which is meagre and hollow, but crisp:
Like a coat that is rather too tight in the waist,
  With a flavour of Will-o'-the-wisp.

"Its habit of getting up late you'll agree
  That it carries too far, when I say
That it frequently breakfasts at five-o'clock tea,
  And dines on the following day.

"The third is its slowness in taking a jest,
  Should you happen to venture on one,
It will sigh like a thing that is deeply distressed:
  And it always looks grave at a pun.

"The fourth is its fondness for bathing-machines.
  Which it constantly carries about,
And believes that they add to the beauty of scenes –
  A sentiment open to doubt.

"The fifth is ambition. It next will be right
  To describe each particular batch:
Distinguishing those that have feathers, and bite,
  From those that have whiskers, and scratch.

"For, although common Snarks do no manner of harm,
  Yet, I feel it my duty to say,
Some are Boojums –" The Bellman broke off in alarm,
  For the Baker had fainted away.

When Baker comes to, he tells the others about his uncle's advice:

"He remarked to me then," said that mildest of men,
  " 'If your Snark be a Snark, that is right:
Fetch it home by all means – you may serve it with greens,
  And it's handy for striking a light.

" 'You may seek it with thimbles – and seek it with care;
  You may hunt it with forks and hope;
You may threaten its life with a railway-share;
  You may charm it with smiles and soap –' "

("That's exactly the method," the Bellman bold
  In a hasty parenthesis cried,
"That's exactly the way I have always been told
  That the capture of Snarks should be tried!")

> " 'But oh, beamish nephew, beware of the day,
>   If your Snark be a Boojum! For then
> You will softly and suddenly vanish away,
>   And never be met with again!'
>
> "It is this, it is this that oppresses my soul,
>   When I think of my uncle's last words:
> And my heart is like nothing so much as a bowl
>   Brimming over with quivering curds!
>
> "It is this, it is this —" "We have had that before!"
>   The Bellman indignantly said.
> And the Baker replied "Let me say it once more.
>   It is this, it is this that I dread!
>
> "I engage with the Snark — every night after dark —
>   In a dreamy delirious fight:
> I serve it with greens in those shadowy scenes,
>   And I use it for striking a light;
>
> "But if ever I meet with a Boojum, that day,
>   In a moment (of this I am sure),
> I shall softly and suddenly vanish away —
>   And the notion I cannot endure!"

It is a sad tale but Bellman reminds them:

> "the Snark is at hand, let me tell you again!
>   'Tis your glorious duty to seek it!
>
> "To seek it with thimbles, to seek it with care;
>   To pursue it with forks and hope;
> To threaten its life with a railway-share;
>   To charm it with smiles and soap!
>
> "For the Snark's a peculiar creature, that won't
>   Be caught in a commonplace way.
> Do all that you know, and try all that you don't:
>   Not a chance must be wasted to-day!
>
> "For England expects — I forbear to proceed:
>   'Tis a maxim tremendous, but trite:
> And you'd best be unpacking the things that you need
>   To rig yourselves out for the fight."

They set out to hunt for the Snark. On the way we learn more about Butcher and Beaver and how their fear of the Jubjub bird made them friends. Then there are two more stories – 'The Barrister's Dream' and Banker's encounter with the Bandersnatch. Finally, in 'The Vanishing', Baker *On the top of a neighbouring crag, Erect and sublime, for one moment of time'* finds a Boojum.

In which strange land do Bellman and the crew hunt for the Snark? On the journey, their boat goes out of control and they only have a blank map to guide them but eventually they land with their *'boxes, portmanteaus, and bags'.*

. . . at first sight the crew were not pleased with the view,
Which consisted of chasms and crags.

During the Second World War, mass bombing raids turned familiar places into strange and desolate landscapes.

The city of Liverpool after eight successive nights of bombing in May 1941. Nineteen hundred people were killed. Forty thousand evacuated themselves to the countyside.

'Everywhere there were piles of rubble and we said "That's Carrington Street, that's the right – no, that's the left side – so we lived there." And then we'd say "Oh no, we lived *there*!" We made to go to our heaps of rubble but, of course, we were stopped. The only thing I was really interested in was my little yellow canary. I was in a terrible state. I couldn't believe that I was in my house. And I found my bird. It had flung him across the floor. I picked him up, he was so black he was like a little sparrow.'

Emma Kitching

LIFE DURING THE BLITZ

The blitz of British cities began with a raid over London on 7 September 1940.

'It was one of those beautiful early autumn days which feel like spring . . . there was hardly a wisp of cloud in the pale blue sky.' *ARP Warden*

Tony Geraghty was living in Pimlico:

'The first surprise was that the enemy was so pretty: fragile silver dragons lit on the slant by a setting sun.' *Sunday Independent*

Living through the raid was a terrifying experience. This record was written in a shelter in Smithy Street, Stepney:

'At 8.15 p.m. a colossal crash, as if the whole street was collapsing, the shelter itself shaking. Immediately, an ARP helper, a nurse, begins singing lustily in an attempt to drown out the noise "Roll out the barrel . . .!" while Mrs S screams "My house! It come on my house! My house is blown to bits!"

There are three more tremendous crashes. Women scream and there is a drawing-together physically. Two sisters clasp one another; women huddle together. There is a feeling of breath being held; everyone waiting for more . . .

People begin shouting at one another. Sophie, thirty, screams at her mother "Oh, you get on my nerves, you do! Oh, shut up, you get on my nerves."'

'The whole of that night was almost as bright as a sunny day.'
Dean of St Paul's Cathedral

'The sky over London was glorious . . . as though a dozen tropical suns were setting round the horizon . . . everywhere the shells sparkled like Christmas baubles.'
Evelyn Waugh

Bridy McHard was eleven at the time. She lost all her family when their building was hit:

> 'You came to and you drifted away again and you kept shouting "Can anyone hear me?" and eventually I heard a voice saying "We're getting to you, don't worry." I was pulled out by the legs backwards on my face and I actually thought I was in a dustbin. It looked like grey ash you get out of a coal fire. My brother-in-law came up and kept asking my name. "Bridy," I said. "Do you not know me? I'm Bridy".'

Kathleen McConnell was in the same building when it was destroyed by the bomb:

> 'I woke up and to be quite honest I thought I was in bed. I thought the sheets are awful tight somehow and I went to turn and I couldn't and then I pulled at the bedclothes, as I thought, and it was stones and rubble that was in my hands and it was very hot.'

Places were terribly silent after a bomb, before the rescue services arrived. Insides of houses were exposed to view – you could see furniture in upstairs rooms, fireplaces and wallpaper, dangling wires and pipes. Under the rubble people were buried, making no sound.

In a London raid, a school was hit at dinnertime. A local woman recalls:

' . . . it was my painful duty to help by picking up any article I saw unearthed as the men dug. I held aloft a small pink purse. No words were needed. The mother of the child to whom it belonged held out her hand. Her face was so anguished it was frightful to behold. She took it and was led wordlessly away.'

London suffered almost continuous bombing for many months. The raids spread to many other cities and towns in Britain.

' . . . there was my sister-in-law's two shops and the fronts was absolutely shattered. "Well, Bert," I said, "the only thing I can think of is that she must have either been bombed to pieces, or else she's in the house somewhere." He said "I've been right through the house. It hasn't got a door nor anything on it. Right out, everything's out." There was her son, my husband, and his brother, and they was digging for four hours until they found her. They was using their fingers, digging, digging. And when they found her, all the side that caught the blast was all blown out, and this side was perfect. That side was all blown out.'   *Exeter woman*

The blitz brought some bizarre sights – 'corpses' from Madame Tussaud's waxworks were found scattering the road; odd stockings wrapped themselves around the tops of trees and flew like flags; on another branch a bowler hat; and spilled bottles from chemists' shops perfumed the air.

' . . . we strolled and gawped, excited . . . by the magical properties of high explosive: how an entire house might be demolished while the late owner's false teeth smiled serene and secure in a glass on the shelf on the wall of a bathroom that was no longer there.'
Tony Geraghty, Sunday Independent

Everywhere there was the acrid smell of high explosive, seeping gas, and worst of all, the smell of death itself.

BOMBING PLAN

The method of bombing a city was first to find its centre with flares and then to set it burning with showers of incendiary bombs. With the buildings ablaze, planes carrying high explosive bombs had a clear target to aim at. The blast from a bomb could kill people and shatter buildings in a wide radius around the point of explosion. Most powerful in the early raids were the landmines which were huge cylinders, eight feet long and two feet in diameter (250 cm x 60 cm), dropped by parachute. They drifted down silently, sometimes entangling themselves in overhead wires and trees where they dangled and swayed, threatening to fall and explode. The blast from a landmine could throw a train high into the air. But most damage was done by incendiary bombs.

These were about the size of a wine bottle, and packed in containers which opened after leaving the aircraft in order to scatter them over a wide area. The noise of them falling was described by a Liverpool housewife as resembling 'peas being dropped on a dish'. On hitting the ground they ignited with a bright flare which then spread to anything nearby that might burn. If you caught one in time you could smother it or kick it away from danger. Some people collected them for fun but later the Germans added explosive charges to some of them so greater caution had to be used. On the night of 10–11 May 1941, over 86,000 incendiaries fell on London. Many fires were prevented by people on fire-watching duty but the fires that caught hold burned with an appalling destructive force, causing 'flying brands of burning material to whirl in the air like autumn leaves in a storm and, as the windows would by then have been shattered by the heat or blast, fire might travel down a street as fast as a man could walk.'

Another danger was unexploded bombs – 'U.X.B.s'. The one below fell in Brockley, south-east London. After being diffused, the bombs were taken by lorry to the nearest large open space where they were exploded.

THE RELICS OF WAR

'... my son was thrilled to find bits of shrapnel in the garden and went around picking them up.'
Clydebank mother

Some things were more valuable than others. Bernard Kops who lived in Stepney Green remembers being told by his friends:

'That bit's no good – it's from an AA (Ack-Ack) gun, but that's all right – it's from a German bomb.'

A crashed German plane

A woman who lived in Cranbrook, Kent remembers:

'A gang of us toured the countryside on bicycles hoping to be the first on the spot when a German parachuted down ... we were not popular with the police as we were always trying to get souvenirs from crashed planes ... my most treasured relic, and I had boxes of them, was a piece of parachute which "an airman had burned to death in."'

LOOTING

Stealing valuables from bombed-out houses was common. Only trivial things were taken – coal, tinned food, books. Even the rescue workers helped themselves, seeing it as a small reward for their gruesome task. 'Our sergeant says loot as much as you like as long as you're not found out' said one auxiliary fireman.

A Coventry woman came home to find that her son's toys had been stolen. 'I could hate the Germans,' she said, 'but I did not want to hate my own countrymen.'

> '. . . in looking at the contents of a bombed house or shop . . . the things don't belong to anyone . . . picking up a book or a pipe that's blown into the street is almost like picking an apple in a deserted orchard far from any road or house.'
>
> *Ed Murrow*

CARRYING ON NORMALLY

The aim of the German bombing was to instill terror and panic and break the nation's will to fight. The destruction certainly affected people's morale, as found by the Bishop of Winchester, who visited Southampton on the morning of 2 December 1940:

> '. . . the people broken in spirit after the sleepless and awful nights. Everyone who can do so is leaving town . . . everywhere I saw men and women carrying suitcases and bundles, the children clutching some precious doll or toy, struggling to get out of Southampton.'

But generally people adapted to the blitz which, despite the problems and the suffering, brought out new spirit and goodwill.

> '. . . sometimes I feels I can't stand it any more. But it don't do to say so. If I says anything my girls say to me "Stop it, Ma! It's no good saying you can't stand it. You've got to!" My girls is ever so good.'
>
> *Portsmouth woman*

Neighbours joined together to fight fires, clear up the damage, and to repair each other's houses. Being alive seemed more important than money.

Just before the war started, the government organised a large-scale evacuation of young children and mothers from the cities. During the blitz, they offered free travel vouchers to encourage people to move away from the danger areas. Most chose to remain and live with the bombs, adapting to the routine of sleeping in shelters or on tube station platforms. Disrupted services – gas, electricity, transport – were quickly restored, few people missed work, and most cinemas remained open.

But people hated the sound of the sirens, the drone of approaching planes, and most of all the lack of sleep:

'I daren't sleep now. I roam around the house and garden and keep going back to the cellar to report to the others . . . I can't sleep but I don't feel terribly tired – living on nerves I suppose . . . It's tragic to see people with children pouring out of the shelters, tired, cramped and aching from six hours sitting on hard benches.'

With adults feeling the strain, children were left more to their own devices. There could be nothing more dangerous, after all, than an air raid; other risks seemed less important by comparison. Many schools were bombed and lessons were frequently interrupted by air raid warnings. The morning after a raid could be a sad time for many children in school.

'When we went to school, the names would go up on the blackboard – all your friends that had been killed. We used to say a little prayer and hope it would be different the next night, but it wasn't.' *Jean Carberry*

Some found the strain too much to bear and had to be taken to hospital for treatment.

'When they heard distant gunfire, they would sit up in bed and whimper like puppies. One little girl had gone completely dumb through terror and another small child I knew went as stiff as a ramrod every time she heard the sirens. Her face turned scarlet and she opened her mouth to scream but no sound came.' *A nurse in a London children's hospital*

60,595 civilians were killed by enemy action during the war.

86,182 were seriously injured.

200,000 houses were destroyed and about 3,750,000 damaged.

STAGING THE PLAY

THE SET

The play uses three locations – the dig, the allotments and the canal.
Most of the action takes place at the dig, so it should be the central
feature of your set design. If your school hall has a conventional
proscenium arch stage, you could fill the stage space with the dig,
leaving small areas to one side for the other two scenes. Movable rostra
for raising the acting area, or the audience seating, would give you more
interesting staging possibilities. Let's say you have some rostra and
could borrow others – you could then try this arrangement.

Extend the acting area out from the stage and place the dig on two
levels. This will make it bigger and more interesting to look at. Place the
Beaver – Baker scenes at the end of this thrust stage arrangement.
Arrange the audience seating around the acting area as close as possible
to the action. Behind the dig, in front of the rear stage wall, build the
skyline of a row of damaged houses using cardboard painted black. By
lighting the wall to create the effect of sky, the houses will be seen in
silhouette.

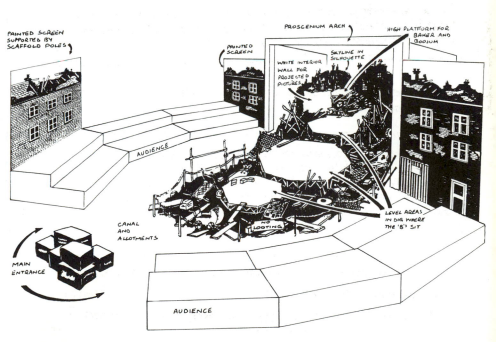

PAINTED SCREEN
SUPPORTED BY
SCAFFOLD POLES

PROSCENIUM ARCH

HIGH PLATFORM FOR
BAKER AND
BOOJUM

PAINTED
SCREEN

SKYLINE IN
SILHOUETTE

WHITE INTERIOR
WALL FOR
PROJECTED
PICTURES

AUDIENCE

CANAL
AND
ALLOTMENTS

NO
LOOTING

LEVEL AREAS
IN DIG WHERE
THE 'B's SIT

MAIN
ENTRANCE

AUDIENCE

Bombing raids left behind great piles of bricks, cement and plaster, but using lots of rubble on the set will be tricky – it's heavy and dirty, and dust from it is likely to be trodden all over the school. While you could use some rubble, try also creating the effects of damage with parts of walls, torn wallpaper, objects strewn around, beams of wood at different angles, wires and old coiled and twisted piping, warning lights and signs. Remember that simple objects tell stories e.g. a child's pram – a reminder of a more peaceful time – where is the child? Is he/she safe?

Build caverns and cavities into the set to make the process of searching more interesting. Do be careful when working on the set – it could be dangerous – things may fall and hurt you, so make sure that everything is secure. Build one large main entrance between the two halves of the audience. This could be used for things like the 'B's' entrance with the wheelbarrow and Butcher's first appearance. Also build concealed entrances in the set to allow people to emerge from the rubble.

Baker will need a safe high point at the top of the dig for when he appears with the Boojum. Consider also the possibility of adding projected images to be set. They could be very effective before the start of the play in setting the atmosphere and landscape of the blitz, especially if accompanied with music of the period or snatches of radio programmes. Rather than add a special screen into the set, project the pictures onto an area of light wallpaper, perhaps with torn edges, which forms part of the set.

After each bombing raid we should see evidence of more destruction. One way of doing this is to remove parts of the set to reveal 'prepared' destruction underneath.

You could also rearrange beams and pipes, remove signs, and for a very special effect, create clouds of 'dust' with a short burst from a smoke machine (in darkness with enough time for the smoke to spread over the set before the lights come up). The hire charge for a machine should not be expensive.

LIGHTING

Keep the set in near darkness when the audience enters to gain full effect when the lights go up. If possible, light the set from a variety of angles. Try experimenting with just one lantern to see how light falls over objects in the set and creates new shapes. Avoid using too much light – shadows are mysterious and dramatic. A good rule to remember is to light only what you want the audience to see. In this play, backlighting will be particularly effective i.e. light shining from behind the actors leaving their faces in shadow.

Try this sequence for the start of the play:

- darkness, sound of bombs, then the all-clear
- dim backlight on dust clouds hanging like mist
- a figure appears in silhouette – it is Bellman
- other figures emerge from the rubble like moles – they look for each other
- more lights fade in revealing the contours of the set but still dim
- from another part of the set the wheelbarrow and the other 'B's appear
- the two groups come together, more light fades in to reveal their faces.

SOUND EFFECTS

The bombs   If you use a recording of an actual raid, you will need a large amplifier and speakers to create the deep thud of the explosions. Be careful not to place them too close to the audience or the effect will be painful.

The approach of the bombers   As often happens with sound in the theatre, you may find that an actual recording of bombers in formation does not sound like the real thing when played back. The sound should *feel* full of menace, doom-laden. You may have more success making your own recording. Try this recording trick. You will need a 2-speed tape recorder and microphone, a large bass drum, and a soft head drum stick. Record a quiet, rapid, continuous beat at the slow speed – 3.75″ per second. Play it back through large speakers at 7.50″ per second with the bass levels up but with the overall levels low. In a dark theatre the effect can be really menacing.

Air raid alert and all-clear   These and other blitz effects – explosions, fire, dive bomb attacks – can be found on BBC Sound Effects record no. 8: RED 126M. Permission should be sought to use these in a public performance. Many record shops stock a good range of sound effects.

Boojum explosion   This should be loud and dramatic. A recorded explosion will be effective only if you have large speakers for the playback. An alternative method is to use a stage maroon. As the maroon creates an actual explosion, it can be DANGEROUS. A competent adult should have sole charge of the set-up and firing of the maroon and the storage of spare maroons.

First, you should obtain the proper equipment from a local theatre hire company. You will need:

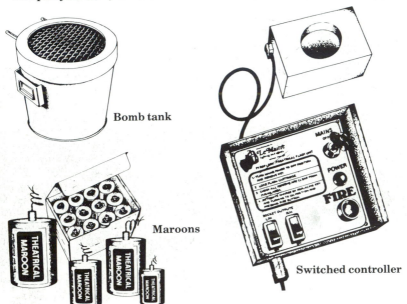

Bomb tank

Maroons

Switched controller

Before using a stage maroon, it is essential that the person in charge studies and follows the *ABTT Code of Practice for the use of pyrotechnics*, obtainable from Donmar Limited, 54 Cavell Street, London E1 2HP.

It will be wise to test the device well in advance with all the cast present, to help you get used to the bang, and to see if the effect works. You may find that the most dramatic effect is the maroon, and a recorded explosion 'fired' at the same moment.

Other sounds, not mentioned in the script, could add atmosphere to your production – popular war-time songs, perhaps, during the interval or between scenes. You can create added tension through contrast e.g. after a fierce raid the first sound we hear over the scene of destruction is the voice of Vera Lynn (the Forces' sweetheart) from a distant radio singing 'There's a New World Over the Skyline'.

Sounds in the play should be carefully integrated into the action e.g. when Butcher threatens to sew up Beaver's mouth, he does it to the sound of approaching planes. The dramatic effect depends on an interplay between the two types of threat. Allow rehearsal time for linking the sound with the action.

COSTUME

These pictures from the television production give you some starting ideas for how the characters should look. Things like the type of glasses and hairstyle are important. Some of the 'B's may carry gas masks. The work that the 'B's have been doing at the dig should be reflected in the way they look.

CREATING THE CHARACTERS

All the characters in the 'B's are very different from each other, both in the way they look and the way they behave. Once you know which character you will be playing, jot down as many details as you can about the character from what he/she says and does in the play. Here are a few starting lists:

Bellman
- likes to be in charge
- enjoys giving orders, making decisions, sorting out jobs
- goes on about discipline, rules
- thinks he's playing an important part in the war effort
- a bit like a sergeant or ARP warden; makes the purpose of the 'B's clear
- has some silly ideas – hit the snark with a hammer – suicide mission?
- threatened by Butcher

Beaver
- embarrassed about his harelip; keeps away from the main scene of the action
- Dad's on convoys

- Mum makes home-made jam
- generous to Baker – gives him Mr Hodges' glass eye
- terrified of Butcher
- shows courage during air raid
- sees acceptance by Butcher as protection for himself

Beryl

- a bully; taunts anybody weaker than herself
- physically strong – really hurts when she punches and is likely to get carried away
- humiliates Barmy
- can't take a joke against herself
- fiercely protective of her mother
- violence and anger always close to the surface
- her big moment – the story of the fivers
- loyal to Bellman but deserts him when Butcher looks like winning the fight

Butcher

- sinister and vicious towards Beaver
- uses lies and menaces to gain power
- makes rat-like movements
- nerve cracks during the raid – terror, panic; uses aggression to cover up his fear?

Baker

- doesn't know who he is at the start
- makes friends with Beaver – two victims together
- intelligent – learns English quickly
- things become more and more desperate but he gains more control of himself
- betrayed by Beaver – left unprotected

1 Now bring all the characters together in a space, ideally with blocks and rostra to make various levels. Starting with one character and adding others one at a time, build a still picture of the 'B's. How each one looks, and is placed in the picture, should tell us about the relationships between the characters – what they are thinking and feeling about each other. Perhaps the picture is a frozen moment during their hunting at the dig. Discuss the relationships as you build the picture. When it is completed show it to some outside observers and listen to their comments.

2 Separate into individual characters. Focus now on the physical characteristics of your character. Select one aspect you think is typical e.g. Beryl with furrowed eyebrows, Baker with a gaping mouth. Objects can help – Barmy may have thick glasses through which he squints, Bellman a clipboard for listing duties and Snark found. Use this single feature as a starting point for building the whole physical shape of your character. It may help to move, do simple actions, but always let the main physical feature shape the rest. Keep practising so that the shape becomes familiar to you.

3 Try an entrance/exit exercise. Each character in turn enters the acting space, stays in it for a short while, then leaves. The character must have a reason for entering the space, and sustain his/her physical shape till after the exit. Sympathetic feedback from observers can be very constructive – 'Which actions, mannerisms fitted the character?', 'Which could be developed?' The comments provide a sort of mirror for the performer but they must be given with sensitivity and be based on a sound knowledge of the play and its characters.

4 Now more about the background stories of each character. We know only a few things about the lives of the characters outside the 'B's. Try developing their stories, building on what is given in the play (for extra help on Baker turn to page 77). In pairs, but not in role, A asks B questions to expand the information about the character:
● home life
● thoughts about the war, how it has changed their lives
● feelings about other members of the 'B's
Then reverse the questioning – B asks A.

5 Put the story and physical portrayal of the character together. In groups of five or six, 'hot seat' each character in turn. Stay in role to and from the chair. Questions should aim to develop the 'story' of the 'B's. Avoid trick questions to catch people out.

6 Now repeat the first still picture exercise, allowing the work you have done on the physical characteristics of the 'B's and their background stories to influence its structure.

PRACTICAL SUGGESTIONS FOR WORKING ON KEY SCENES

1 Act 1 Scene 1 – The dig

Discovering relationships between the 'B's

Though the 'B's work together as a gang, they don't like each other and relationships between them get worse as the play progresses. The first scene should establish each character and his/her relationship to the rest of the gang before the pressure of events forces change.

(a) After doing the character exercises suggested above, read the scene again. Then divide into groups of six each with Beryl, Baker, Bellman, Barmy, Beaver and Bonkers *or* Billiard Ball.

(b) Try this exercise to help explore their relationships further. You will need two dice, a shaker and six chairs. Sit in a circle with two 'hot-seats'. Number each character – Beryl–1, Baker–2, etc. – around the circle. Throw both dice – the characters whose numbers come up take the 'hot-seats'. (If you get two of the same number, throw again.) The 'hot-seated' characters talk about their relationship with each other helped by questions from the others. Keep throwing the dice till you have dealt with each relationship.

(c) Now arrange some blocks and rostra in the shape of the dig with different levels and flat areas, hidden entrances and hiding places. Bear in mind as you do so where and how the different characters are likely to move in the space.

   Focus on one moment in scene 1 e.g. when the 'B's are trying to find out Baker's name (everybody except Beaver has something to say at this point). Place yourselves on the dig in a way which represents the different relationships in the gang – leaders and followers, bullies and victims. Think carefully about the effects gained by placing characters at the centre or at the edges, on a high or a low level. Where would Bellman like to be to maintain his authority? Which position would make Baker feel threatened? Beaver is out of things but still one of the gang – where should he be in relation to the others?

(d) Work in the same way on another key moment in the scene – when Bellman calls on Beaver to look after Baker and the gang mock him.

(e) Read the whole scene on the set of the dig, stopping where necessary to work out how positions and movements on the set could help to express character relationships.

2 Act 1 Scene 3 and Act 2 Scene 3 – Butcher and the 'B's

Using lights and sound effects to heighten the action

At certain points in the play the drama can be intensified by lights and sound. Two scenes with Butcher and the 'B's lend themselves to extra technical treatment.

70

(a) Act 1 Scene 3 – The arrival of Butcher at the dig

From the way the 'B's talk about Butcher before he arrives we know he is a threatening figure so his arrival must have dramatic impact.

The 'B's are working on the dig. When talking about Butcher they tend to draw closer together for security.

BERYL   Who do you hate most in the world?
BEAVER   Butcher.
BELLMAN   He's back.

Sound: low threatening hum of distant bombers (representing how they all feel about Butcher). Spotlight up on main entrance opposite the dig (shaped as a corridor of light). Butcher enters the light in silhouette. Drone of planes continues. The light focuses attention on Butcher's *shadow*, making him larger than life. The narrators speak. Drone of planes increases. Lights on the dig narrow to Bellman – with Beryl and Baker on the edges. Butcher and Bellman confront each other across the distance. A tense stillness with the sound of approaching planes. The narrators speak again. Beaver makes a sudden dash

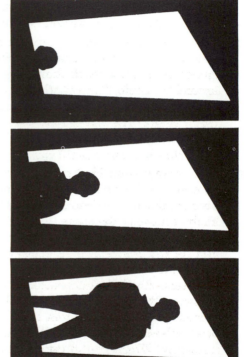

out of the shadows past Butcher but Butcher catches him effortlessly. Screams, whimpers from Beaver. A dull thud of a bomb dropping in the distance . . .

Once you have established the tension of Butcher's entry, try to sustain it to the end of the scene when the bombs are almost overhead.

(b) Act 2 Scene 3 – Butcher's breakdown

Sound: bombs exploding in the distance.

Butcher sits in the deckchair. The bombs get closer and louder. As they do so, the lights change to a single bright spot above Butcher as if to make him a clearer target for the bombers.

(Beaver can be seen close by in the reflected light, sifting through the rubble).

Butcher looks up to the planes above. His fear becomes 'white hot' like the light on his face.

The sound of a single bomb dropping (a stylised sound created live with electronic instruments may be more effective than a recording of an actual bomb).

Just before the explosion Butcher screams out hysterically, gripping onto the chair, unable to take his eyes off the falling bombs.

Explosion – blackout.

Falling debris – silence.

Slowly fade up back light to dim. Through the dust and shadow we make out Beaver cradling a sobbing Butcher.

3 Act 2 Scene 2 – The canal

Changing the atmosphere between scenes

In scene 2, Beaver and Baker are fishing in the canal. The atmosphere in this scene is quite different from the dig. Away from the bombs and the taunts of the other 'B's, they can talk more freely. The 'B's rarely drop their guard with each other but here Beaver and Baker share the sort of experiences that build friendship and trust.

As preparation for working on the scene, think back to an experience in your own life which you found embarrassing and, perhaps, difficult to talk about. Ask yourself – when did it happen? Who was there? What did you think and feel at the time? Of all the people you know, who would you find it easiest to talk to about it? Perhaps nobody at all. You may wish to try telling yourself about it by writing it down. Nobody need see what you write; just putting the experience into words can help you to understand it better.

When creating scene 2 in action, think about:

● how to create atmosphere with sound – lapping water, birdsong high above (very quiet so as not to intrude)
● silences – this is a scene when characters are thinking inner thoughts as well as speaking; they don't need to talk all the time

- how Baker works his way around to telling his secret story – this cannot be easy for him because he risks embarrassing himself
- the audience – by building pauses into the scene, you give them time to think about what is going on inside the characters' heads

4 Act 2 Scene 4 – Baker is accused of stealing the money
Drawing out dramatic tensions
Every play has special moments of high dramatic tension. When building a production it is important to know where these may be. Each part of the play builds towards one of these tensions. This is how scenes find a sense of direction.

We have discussed some special points of tension already – Baker's initiation into the 'B's, Butcher's arrival etc. The most significant changes are those which bring about changes in character relationships. Look at scene 4 and the business of the money-box – Banker and Barrister have framed Baker. Bellman opens the box, Baker is accused of stealing the money, Butcher gives false witness and Beaver betrays Baker. The scene draws into focus lots of issues in the play – the problems of keeping rules and order, being honest and loyal, struggles for the leadership and the developing friendship between Baker and Beaver.

The most important moment in the scene is Beaver's betrayal of Baker. For it is this that makes Baker realise he is completely alone, without friends or family. From now on he will need the Snark to defend himself from everybody around him. Dramatically, the focus should be on Beaver's silent agony – should he speak the truth and stay loyal to Baker or give into pressure and win protection from Butcher? The moment is made dramatic *by the way the scene builds towards it.*

These director's notes give you some practical ideas on how to create the dramatic tension step by step.

Beaver at side, front of stage, away from Baker and the 'B's

B's have been taunting Barny to this point. Prospect of money diverts their interest

Butcher observes everything from the top of the dig offers the box innocently

Banker and Barrister on opposite sides of dig. We can see they are up to something

anger of feeling cheated, 'B's ready to accuse

pretending he knows nothing

BELLMAN	Now let's get on. Where's Banker? Time for the count out.
BAKER	He's not coming. He's at his nephew's chiselling.
BEAVER	*(correcting)* Christening.
BAKER	I have the money-box.
BELLMAN	And I have the key. Right, put it down here and I'll open it.

Bellman opens the box. There is immediate consternation. It is full of stones and bits of torn-up newspaper. The kids ad lib their anger. In a corner Barrister beckons to Banker who comes running on. As Banker passes they give each other a sly 'thumbs up' sign.

BANKER	*(running on)* Sorry I'm late. Well, how much then?
BERYL	Nothing! It's been stolen! This box is full of torn paper and stones.

73

The annotations on the left (handwritten):

- Banker directs the 'B's' anger towards Baker
- Baker suddenly on 'hot-spot' - centre stage - surrounded by others ⓑ
- makes it like a mock court
- plays to the 'gallery' - The 'B's fall for it
- threatens violence - support from the 'mob'
- higher than the others (judge?) - trying to keep order
- PAUSE before Beaver speaks - his voice heard from outside the centre of action
- really desperate now (tears)
- 'No' follows 'Yes' - as if on the next musical beat
- PAUSE as attention shifts up the dig to Butcher. He walks down through the 'B's to Beaver, who is facing away
- close to Beaver now - speaking like a 'friend'
- feels pressure of Butcher's presence. Does not look at him
- menacing 'friendly' tone (hand on shoulder)
- Butcher walks over to Baker - speaks these lines directly to Baker's face
- PAUSE Butcher's stare fixed on Baker Another PAUSE
- Butcher turns to Beaver
- Beaver turns to gang PAUSE
- all the gang turn towards Beaver LONG PAUSE
- Releases 'B's' anger towards Baker

BANKER	Empty? Empty? (*He suddenly grabs* **Baker** *by his lapels*) You thief! What have you done with our money?

The others group round them.

BAKER	What? What? I haven't taken the money.
BARRISTER	Have you any grounds for this allegation, Banker?
BANKER	I certainly have, Barrister. This box was full of money when I gave it to him last night. Now it's empty. It stands to reason he's been at it.
BAKER	What about you? Maybe you gave me a box full of stones and paper.

Banker *goes for* **Baker**.

BANKER	I'll have him! He's calling me a thief!
BAKER	(*desperately*) You're calling me one.
BELLMAN	Look, are there any witnesses?
BEAVER	I saw Banker give Baker the money-box.
BELLMAN	And did he go straight home?
BEAVER	I think so.
BAKER	Yes!
BUTCHER	No! (*to* **Beaver**) Don't you remember – we saw him come creeping back again.
BAKER	No! I went straight home!
BELLMAN	Be quiet.
BERYL	Shut it!
BUTCHER	(*to* **Beaver**) You remember – he didn't see us. He squatted down just over there, didn't he?
BAKER	It's a lie!
BELLMAN	Go on.
BUTCHER	(*to* **Beaver**) What happened then?
BEAVER	I don't remember.
BUTCHER	Yes, you do. He got out a great bunch of keys.
BAKER	I don't have any keys!
BILLIARD	He's hidden them again.
BUTCHER	I said to Beaver, 'What's he up to?' and Beaver said, 'Counting his money, Jews always have money.' That's what you said, didn't you?
BELLMAN	(*to* **Beaver**) Well?
BARRISTER	Well, Beaver?
BUTCHER	Well, Beaver? Tell the truth. You did say that, didn't you?

Beaver *stands silently, in agony. Finally, he's nearly one of the gang but the price is betraying* **Baker**. *He gives up the struggle and says what they want to hear.*

BEAVER	Yes.
BAKER	(*appalled at* **Beaver**) Liar, liar.
BARRISTER	Right, that's that. He's guilty!

Beaver, alone, doubles up with the agony he is feeling

5 Act 2 Scene 4 – The arrival of the telegram boy
Act 2 Scene 5 – Baker's entry with the Boojum

Building group images

To make the play dramatically effective you need to know what your character is thinking and feeling and the reasons for his/her behaviour. But certain moments in the play will depend for their effect on carefully constructed images using the whole group. For these you will need to work more as a sculptor, placing each person and timing movements to create just the effect you want.

Here are examples of how you might approach two such moments:

(a) Act 2 Scene 4 – The telegram boy

*The '**B**'s are on the dig, fairly close together.*

BERYL   *(shouts from the rear)* Quiet.

Everybody becomes still and listens. Silence. A creaking sound – very distant. We are not yet sure what it is. **Beryl** *turns to the rear.*

BERYL   It's the telegram boy.

Sound still distant.

BOOTS   Don't let him turn down our street.

The gang tense and still.

BERYL   He's in it already.

Creaking sound gets louder from the rear. They look towards the sound and, turning slowly, they watch the 'boy' cycle between them and the audience (this will need practice – all eyes must follow the same moving spot). In doing so, they turn to the front, creating a cluster of faces.

This can be a powerful image – we 'watch' the telegram boy through the reactions on the faces. Make sure they are well lit, perhaps focusing light *only* on the faces. Keep the image still, except for the relief shown on one or two faces when the boy passes their house (the contrast in movement creates the drama). But when Brains realises it is his house, he could be the one to remain motionless while the others turn towards him or move away.

The tendency is to rush moments like this. It works best when each person is paying close attention to everybody else in the scene and sensing the dramatic tension.

(b) Act 2 Scene 5 – Baker and the Boojum

Just before the explosion, Baker enjoys a moment of triumph. He could appear high up on the dig holding the bomb above his head. The 'B's, responding to Beaver's shouts, then enter opposite and, amazed at what they see, take up positions around the set facing Baker. By placing a very strong light behind Baker, directed towards the audience, you will cast both his figure and the gang in a stark silhouette. Use the brightest light you have got. If you have a white expanse of backdrop behind the dig you could add to the first light a fan of different colours projected upwards on the backdrop. The effect will be something like the representation of a moment of glory you sometimes see in a comic or picture book.

BAKER'S STORY

When Baker first appears in the story he is weak and pathetic. He looks stupid dressed in all his coats and when the others ask him his name, he can't remember it. Whatever they suggest he goes along with and he is too feeble to put up any resistance to Beryl's bullying. Later, we learn that his mother has had a mental breakdown and, with no family left, he is put into a home. Even Beaver, his only friend, betrays him.

Is Baker really a weak character? Or has the war made him a victim? Baker himself gives us some clues – he and his mother had to leave Poland in a great hurry, his father has disappeared, all their possessions are lost. Then, in the allotments, he says some chilling words to Beaver. 'When the words no longer hurt you, then they'll beat you. When you don't feel any more pain, then they'll kill you.' Beaver thinks he's 'bonkers'. More likely though that Baker, as a refugee, has been living in terror since long before the war, and that when he first meets the 'B's he is in a state of shock. What is his story?

Baker is a Jew. Long before the war started the Jews of Europe suffered terror, hostility and discrimination at the hands of the German Nazis. They were driven out of their jobs; signs were daubed on their shops 'JEWS OUT'; houses were vandalised and their contents burned on bonfires in the streets. Many thousands were imprisoned without reason in concentration camps. Hitler hated the Jews, believing them to be corrupters of the Germanic people who were of pure 'Aryan' descent, so he

German Jewish refugees

claimed. In the years before the war, this hatred spread like a disease.

The German forces invaded Poland on 1 September 1939. In every village Nazi soldiers forced Jews to carry heavy loads, to hand over gold and silver and to clean floors and lavatories with their prayer shawls.

'. . . it was a Friday night. It had been quiet in town for a few days. I wanted to go out. My mother said "No" but I pleaded with her and she agreed, but with a warning. I walked past a few houses – all was quiet.

Then, from nowhere, a German soldier appeared in front of me.

"Are you a Jew?"

"Yes, I am a Jew."

As soon as I said the word "Jew" he started beating me with his hands, then he took his gun and beat me on the back with the butt. After that he put me against the wall and aimed the gun at me. "I'm going to kill you, dirty Jew." He was laughing when he said it. Just then a woman ran out of her house and begged him to stop. She was on her knees at his feet, pleading. He paused, then put the gun back on his shoulder and said, "Fast, *schnell!* Go home, dirty Jew and Polish pig." *Yitzhak Steinblat*

Five thousand Jews died in Poland in September and October 1939. Those that survived lived in constant fear. David Wdowinski worked in a hospital in Warsaw.

'. . . they demanded money, jewels, goods and food. They shut the women up in one room and the men in another. They stole everything they could lay their hands on and ordered the men to load it onto the trucks, to the accompaniment of kicks and beatings . . . suddenly one of the officers noticed a small medallion round the neck of a little boy. This child had been ill from birth . . . the only thing that gave him comfort in any way was this medallion. In the presence of the officers this child was taken with a seizure and the mother pleaded that the medallion be left for her child. One of the officers watching the child said: "I see that the child is ill. I am a doctor, but a Jew-kid is not a human being," and he tore the medallion off the neck of the boy.'

In the following year the ghettos were established. These were areas of towns and cities in which all the Jews were forced to live. Families were crammed in with whatever possessions they could bring with them. Food was desperately short, and in the winter the cold was intense. High walls circled the ghettos to prevent escape. Worst of all was the constant threat of violence and death. Avraham Aviel, who was then fourteen, remembers one of the days when the soldiers arrived.

'I tried to hide my smaller brother and my mother and the people who were with us in the house. I tried to hide them in the attic. I covered them with rags and boxes, then I went down and I tried to find out what was happening. As soon as I came down from the attic, I heard a terrible noise. Motorcycles were coming in. There were shouts. Germans came in from the direction of Lida in battle uniform equipped with automatic weapons as if they were marching out to the front . . . I left the house and I saw a great mass of Jews being pushed from the edge of the ghetto, being driven in the direction of Grodno. The same direction in which these groups with the spades had been going. And then we knew that something dreadful was going to happen.'

Jan Ciechanowski was a member of the Polish resistance movement, though only twelve years old. Not being a Jew he could move more freely around the city. He carried messages, weapons and helped people in the ghetto by bringing in food through holes in the wall. Then one sunny morning, when standing on the balcony of his uncle's house:

'. . . I witnessed the worst thing I ever saw in my whole life. German police arrived and surrounded the ghetto . . . they began marching off into the stations columns of Jews carrying little bundles, the parents holding the children's hands. I then saw a smaller column of old people and toddlers being led in the opposite direction, towards a clearing in the wood. A lot of shots rang out from there. Two more little crocodiles of youngest and oldest were each followed by a volley of shots . . . afterwards, some lorryloads of German police drove out of the clearing and stopped quite near me . . . they were joking and drinking cool fizzy drinks . . . some wore oilskin butchers' aprons. Most looked between thirty and forty and I thought they might well be fathers themselves. I don't have words for what I felt. I wanted to be sick. I gazed at them in horror unable to understand why.'

SS Sergeant Felix Landau, in charge of many of these executions, wrote in his diary:

14 July 1941

We drive a few kilometres along the main road till we reach a wood. We go into the wood and look for a spot suitable for mass executions. We order the prisoners to dig their graves. Only two of them are crying. The others show courage. What can they be thinking? I believe each still has the hope of not being shot. I don't feel the slightest stir of pity. That's how it is, and has got to be.

28 July 1941

. . . they collapse on top of one another - they scream like pigs - we stand and look on. Who gave the orders to kill the Jews? No one! Somebody ordered them to be set free. They were all murdered because we hate them.

But many Jews escaped from the ghettos. When the opportunity came they had to leave everything. Here is an episode from the story of Bronia Spira and her son Yitzhak. Unlike most Jews, Bronia had fair hair and blue eyes, and because of them she had managed to obtain false 'Aryan' papers and to conceal her Jewish identity. Yitzhak was also fair but spoke with a Jewish accent which could give the game away. Bronia and Yitzhak were travelling on a train next to two German soldiers. Yitzhak was asleep with his head on his mother's lap. Bronia tells the story.

'The two German officers started to talk with me, and before long got round to discussing their favourite topic – the Jews. Their language was brutal and vulgar, although they apologised to me for speaking that way in the presence of a lady. Then one officer recalled how on a similar journey he had discovered a Jew who was travelling on "Aryan" papers. "I sniffed him out," he said, "I have a special talent for it. I made him pull down his trousers in the middle of the compartment. I was right. The poor devil never made it to the next station." He laughed when he told the story, trying to amuse me. I thought about Yitzhak and my heart pounded. I prayed that he would not wake up. I smiled at them and said, "Gentlemen, you don't want to wake up a future soldier." They looked at Yitzhak and smiled. "You remind me of the beautiful madonna and child in my village, Saint Ottilier," one of them said. From then on they talked in hushed voices.'

> **Fifty thousand Jews found safety from the Nazi terror in Britain**

These accounts give you a basis for working out what might have happened to Baker before the play starts. Work in small groups – no more than three or four in each. Before you begin devising the story you may wish to do further research – do not feel limited by the stories given. You should find these books helpful:

The Third Reich by David Williamson, Witness History Series, Wayland, 1988; *Nazi Germany* by Stephen Lee, Heinemann, 1989; *Hitler's Germany, Germany 1933–45* by Josh Brooman, Longman 1985; *The Holocaust* by Martin Gilbert, Collins, 1986; *The Diary of Anne Frank*, Pan Books, 1989.

First ask yourselves some questions:

- What was life like in the Polish village for Baker and his family before the Germans arrived?
- How did they live in the ghetto? Try to picture the house they shared with many other families.
- What 'incidents' did they witness in the ghetto?
- Perhaps Jan, the resistance fighter, helped them to escape. If so, how did he do it?
- What about the moment when Baker was separated from his father – what was happening? Who was there?
- Did any other incidents occur on the journey to England? Remember that at each border crossing their papers would be checked.

Once you have worked out the story, you could use it to create a simple but very effective performance. Rather than attempt to act it all out, which will take a lot of time and people, build the performance with just two dramatic techniques:

1 *Talking heads*   This is when a character from a particular situation speaks directly to the audience about what happened and who was there, what he/she was thinking at the time. A talking head is not a narrator putting a whole story together but simply a character talking from inside a situation as he/she sees it.

2 *Tableaux*   These are still pictures depicting key moments in the story. The talking heads may be linked directly with the pictures.

Think carefully about which characters in your story should speak. It might be a good idea *not* to include Baker or his mother, or indeed to have a narrator. Assume that the audience knows something of Baker and his mother from the play, then choose the characters and moments that will give a special insight into the story and leave the audience to make some of the connections with Baker for themselves. There are plenty of characters (some 'hidden') in the stories to get you started:

- the woman who pleaded for Yitzhak's release
- a soldier who has just entered a house in the ghetto but failed to find people he knows are hiding there
- a friend of Jan's describing what happened to him when the Germans discovered he had helped a Jewish family to escape
- somebody on the train who watched Bronia with her son and has suspicions.

BUTCHER AND BEAVER
AND THE JUBJUB BIRD

Butcher seems to be the strongest of the 'B's. They are all frightened of him. He terrorises Beaver and he beats Bellman in a fight to become leader. But during the second air raid, fear gets the better of him and he breaks down in tears. Beaver feels he has never been fully accepted by the gang and is the butt of all their jokes. But in the face of danger from the bombs he shows unexpected courage and this changes his relationship with Butcher. One moment Butcher shows hatred towards Beaver, attacking him with abuse and physical threats. The next, he calls him 'me old mate, Beaver' in front of the other 'B's. Why this change in Butcher?

During the Second World War, many people felt that the danger somehow brought out the best in them. To be alive was, after all, the most important thing and friendship counted for more than power and possessions. Butcher may, of course, have made Beaver his friend to protect himself. He wouldn't want the 'B's to know about his breakdown during the air raid. But the bombs certainly changed him. Sometimes strong feelings do change suddenly and sworn enemies become the best of friends but how it happens is rather puzzling and mysterious.

You could look at this special relationship between Butcher and Beaver through a small separate performance project which combines scenes from the play and new sections of the poem. A group of seven or eight might work on this together, as an independent production that is linked with the play.

In the fifth part of Lewis Carroll's *The Hunting of the Snark* Butcher and Beaver, each following his own plan to find the Snark, meet by coincidence in a '*dismal and desolate valley*' where they hear the dreaded scream of the Jubjub Bird. The Beaver '*turned pale to the tip of his tail, And even the Butcher felt queer*'. But in coping with their fear they become good friends. By integrating sections of the poem with the Butcher and Beaver scenes from the play you could build a new drama focusing on their relationship and the bomb terror that changes it. The Jubjub Bird in the poem represents danger and threat. The bombers could be Jubjub Birds that '*scream shrill and high*' and '*rend the shuddering sky*'. It will be a good idea to read the sections of the poem on the following pages before beginning work on the project. Afterwards, you will need to construct a sequence using sections of both the poem and the play. Here is one way of building a sequence.

First you bring together the two main scenes with Butcher and Beaver.

Act One Second half of Scene 3 – The arrival of Butcher	Act Two Second half of Scene 3 – The air raid

Then insert extended sections of the poem at key points.

1 Begin at the moment on page 18 when Butcher appears during the air raid siren. (See page 71 for ideas on staging Butcher's entry.)

> *He came as a butcher: but gravely declared*
>> *When the ship had been sailing a week,*
> *He could only kill Beavers. The Bellman looked scared,*
>> *And was almost too frightened to speak . . .*

Stick to the script from here through to the point on page 20 when the gang run away from the falling bombs (in this section, Butcher goes for Beaver, calling him a deformed cripple and a monster. Just to look at his face makes him sick, and he threatens to sew up his mouth with needle and cotton.) When Bellman shouts 'Run', all the gang rush off leaving Butcher and Beaver glaring at each other, with Baker watching at a distance.

2 *Then the butcher contrived an ingenious plan*
>> *For making a separate sally;*
> *And had fixed on a spot unfrequented by man,*
>> *A dismal and desolate valley.*

> *But the very same plan to the Beaver occurred:*
>> *It had chosen the very same place;*
> *Yet neither betrayed, by a sign or a word,*
>> *The disgust that appeared in his face.*

> *Each thought he was thinking of nothing but "Snark"*
>> *And the glorious work of the day;*
> *And each tried to pretend that he did not remark*
>> *That the other was going that way.*

> *But the valley grew narrow and narrower still,*
>> *And the evening got darker and colder,*
> *Till (merely from nervousness, not from goodwill)*
>> *They marched along shoulder to shoulder.*

Then a scream, shrill and high, rent the shuddering sky,
  And they knew that some danger was near:
The Beaver turned pale to the tip of its tail,
  And even the Butcher felt queer.

He thought of his childhood, left far far behind —
  That blissful and innocent state —
The sound so exactly recalled to his mind
  A pencil that squeaks on a slate!

" 'Tis the voice of the Jubjub!" he suddenly cried.
  (This man, that they used to call "Dunce".)
"As the Bellman would tell you," he added with pride,
  "I have uttered that sentiment once.

" 'Tis the note of the Jubjub! Keep count, I entreat;
  You will find I have told it you twice.
'Tis the song of the Jubjub! The proof is complete,
  If only I've stated it thrice."

The Beaver had counted with scrupulous care,
  Attending to every word:
But it fairly lost heart, and outgrabe in despair,
  When the third repetition occurred.

As the verses are spoken the sound of bombers gets gradually louder. All the while Butcher menaces Beaver with his very presence. The sound and the action build to a powerful tension.

3 While sustaining the tension, cut to the second air raid on page 35, and Baker's line 'There are going to be bombs.' (The business of Banker and the money-box is not important in this short play where the focus is on Beaver and Butcher, so you could leave it out.) Butcher says he'll stay for the fireworks. Beaver says he'll stay with him. Follow the script till Beaver says 'You settle down in the deckchair and watch the display.' They sit down.

4 *"As to temper the Jubjub's a desperate bird,*
 Since it lives in perpetual passion:
Its taste in costume is entirely absurd –
 It is ages ahead of the fashion:

"But it knows any friend it has met once before:
 It never will look at a bribe:
And in charity meetings it stands at the door,
 And collects – though it does not subscribe.

"Its flavour when cooked is more exquisite far
 Than mutton, or oysters, or eggs:
(Some think it keeps best in an ivory jar,
 And some, in mahogany kegs:)

"You boil it in sawdust: you salt it in glue:
 You condense it with locusts and tape:
Still keeping one principal object in view –
 To preserve its symmetrical shape."

The menacing sound of the bombers steadily increases with each verse. Cut back to the text.

5 BEAVER   I won't disturb you over there, will I?

Bombs start to drop. They get closer and closer. Butcher breaks down in hysterics. Beaver comforts him.

BEAVER   It's all right – it's all right me old mate. I'm here, I'm here.

(For further ideas on staging this section see page 72.)

6 *The Butcher would gladly have talked till next day,*
 But he felt that the Lesson must end,
And he wept with delight in attempting to say
 He considered the Beaver his friend.

While the Beaver confessed, with affectionate looks
 More eloquent even than tears,
It had learnt in ten minutes far more than all books
 Would have taught it in seventy years.

They returned hand-in-hand, and the Bellman, unmanned
  (For a moment) with noble emotion,
Said "This amply repays all the wearisome days
  We have spent on the billowy ocean!"

Such friends, as the Beaver and Butcher became,
  Have seldom if ever been known;
In winter or summer, 'twas always the same –
  You could never meet either alone.

And when quarrels arose – as one frequently finds
  Quarrels will, spite of every endeavour –
The song of the Jubjub recurred to their minds,
  And cemented their friendship for ever!

To perform this project you will need only a small space without any set. Place the audience as close as you can to the acting area – if possible, on all four sides. This will help to create an intimate atmosphere and focus attention on the two main characters. Add some lights if you can but, most importantly, make sure that the sounds of the air raid create the effect you want. The audience should share Butcher's fear of the bombers. (See page 65 for more advice on sound effects.)

Narrators – again they will probably be most effective close to the action. Try placing them in the corners of the acting space in line with the front row of the audience. From there they will be able to speak quietly (in whispers, if you like) and draw the audience into the story. They could speak across the space to each other or together in chorus. In the way that they relate to both the action and the audience try to develop the contrast and tension between the nonsensical images in the poem and the horror of the event taking place before them.

THE BOOJUM
A SHORT PLAY FOR RADIO

The play *The Hunting of the Snark* would work well as a radio drama. It uses many different types of sounds which could create strong pictures of war and desolation in the imagination of the listener and, apart from certain visual dramatic moments, such as the arrival of the telegram boy, the dialogue gives us a clear sense of the action.

Two things you will need to bear in mind from the start:

1 The different personalities of the characters will be expressed through their voices – their sound and intonation.

2 Sound effects and dialogue should be carefully integrated so do plenty of experimental recordings to get the quality of sound you want.

As recording a play for radio is technically quite complicated, it will probably be a good idea to work on just a short section of the text. A good part to try would be the final scene when Baker finds the Boojum. It has a strong dramatic focus with special sound effects – passing bombers, exploding Boojum, and a variety of voices.

Probably the most straightforward way of creating the play will be to stick faithfully to the text of the scene. But you may find it more fun to change the setting of the play. The 'B's' story is a drama about human relationships and survival amidst destruction and chaos which could easily be set in a different place and time. Remember – you won't have the complication of building a stage set and working with sound gives you freedom – you can establish a location with just a simple sound effect.

One possibility is to set the play in the future during a different kind of war. Instead of World War II bombers, air raid sirens and bombs, you could use radiophonic sounds and synthesisers to suggest an unfamiliar environment desolated by war. Some of the other worldly sounds that electronic instruments make would fit well with the strange world of the poem *The Hunting of the Snark*. Look at the landscape of '*chasms and crags*' on pages 54–5. How could you represent it in sound? This might be a good starting exercise.

Here is a scenario based on the final scene of the play. It uses all the verses in 'The Vanishing', the last section of Lewis Carroll's poem. Although the scenario is broken down into sections, the scene should flow continuously on playback.

These records will provide you with some of the sound effects you may need.

1 **Hi-Tech FX** – sounds of space; intergalactic battle; rocket flights. BBC REC 531 Stereo.

2 **Radiophonic music** – electronic atmospheres. BBC REC 25M.

3 **Out of this world** – desolate environments; futuristic machines. BBC REC 225.

THE BOOJUM

1 Fade in sounds depicting a futuristic landscape with, perhaps, hot dust storms, hurtling spacecraft, and muffled explosions in the distance. (Keep these sounds going in the background right through to the explosion of the Boojum.)

2 Mix in a melody played on an electronic instrument – something slightly weird but tuneful, to contrast with the atmospheric sounds. Continue both sounds through the spoken verses. Try to give the voices an eerie quality. You could record them in a room that makes echoes or with one voice whispering close to the microphone.

3 *They sought it with thimbles, they sought it with care;*
   They pursued it with forks and hope;
They threatened its life with a railway-share;
   They charmed it with smiles and soap.

They shuddered to think that the chase might fail,
   And the Beaver, excited at last,
Went bounding along on the tip of its tail,
   For the daylight was nearly past.

4 Sounds close to of someone moving stones, rubble, as if searching.
   BEAVER   *(distant)* I thought you'd gone.
   BAKER   *(close)* No.
   BEAVER   *(coming closer)* Someone said you had.

   Continue the dialogue between Beaver and Baker, leaving time during the pauses for the listener to pick up the atmospheric sounds again. (Change any words which feel out of place e.g. 'bike', 'jam' and add other words and lines you feel will add to the futuristic setting.)

5 Baker goes frantic seeing a 'vision of death' coming towards him. Mix in the melody we heard soon after the beginning. The contrast of words and music should increase the effect of Baker's desperation.

6 Beaver helps Baker search through the rubble. More frantic now. Fade in the menacing drone of approaching aircraft (a bunch of low notes on a synthesiser turned up gradually on the volume control to simulate their approach).

BAKER	*(more distant)* I've looked over there.
BEAVER	*(close)* What about about the top?
BAKER	No.
BEAVER	We'll start there.

More digging. Aircraft sounds increase, then fade as they pass overhead. Long yell of triumph from **Baker** *(very distant)*.

BEAVER	*(also distant)* He's done it! He's found one! He's found a Snark!

7 The melody again and voices close to. In these verses use the contrasting voices of different characters. Try to get the effect of a huddle of people close to the listener watching Baker in the distance.

"There is Thingumbob shouting!" the Bellman said.
  "He is shouting like mad, only hark!
He is waving his hands, he is wagging his head,
  He has certainly found a Snark!"

They gazed in delight, while the Butcher exclaimed
  "He was always a desperate wag!"
They beheld him – their Baker – their hero unnamed –
  On the top of a neighbouring crag.

Erect and sublime, for one moment of time.
  In the next, that wild figure they saw
(As if stung by a spasm) plunge into a chasm,
  While they waited and listened in awe.

"It's a Snark!" was the sound that first came to their ears,
  And seemed almost too good to be true.
Then followed a torrent of laughter and cheers:
  Then the ominous words "It's a Boo –"

8 Dialogue suddenly sounds more realistic.

BAKER	*(distant)*: Get away!! Go! Get away!!
BEAVER	They've come to help, Baker.
BAKER	*(urgently)* You don't understand – it's started to tick – it's a Boo . . .

9 Sound of an explosion as if from a far crag.

10 After it has died away six seconds silence.

Then, silence. Some fancied they heard in the air
  A weary and wandering sigh
That sounded like "– jum!" but the others declare
  It was only a breeze that went by.

11 Fade in atmospheric sounds. Mix in the now familiar melody during the verses.

> *They hunted till darkness came on, but they found*
> *Not a button, or feather, or mark,*
> *By which they could tell that they stood on the ground*
> *Where the Baker had met with the Snark.*
>
> *In the midst of the word he was trying to say,*
> *In the midst of his laughter and glee,*
> *He had softly and suddenly vanished away –*
> *For the Snark was a Boojum, you see.*

12 Sounds fade. Atmospheric sounds first, leaving the melody which then slow fades to silence.